Go ahead and scream.

No one can hear you. You're no longer in the safe world you know.

You've taken a terrifying step . . .

into the darkest corners of your imagination.

You've opened the door to . . .

the NIGHTMARE room

Locker 13

R. L. STINE

AVON BOOKS

An Imprint of HarperCollins*Publishers*

Locker 13

Special Thanks to Mr. George Sheanshang

Printed in the United States of America.

For information address:
HarperCollins Children's Books,
a division of HarperCollins Publishers,
1350 Avenue of the Americas,
New York, NY 10019.

Library of Congress Catalog Card Number: 00-190244
ISBN 0-06-440900-7

First Avon edition, 2000

Visit us on the World Wide Web!
www.harperchildrens.com

Welcome...

I'm R.L. Stine, and I want to introduce you to Luke Greene. He's that short, wiry seventh-grader standing in front of his locker.

Some kids tease Luke about being too superstitious. He wears a lucky shirt to school, and he never goes anywhere without a lucky rabbit's foot tucked in his pocket.

Luke doesn't mind being teased. He says you can never have enough good luck.

That's why he's so unhappy about his new locker. It's the first day of school, and Luke has been given Locker 13.

Luke is staring at the locker in horror—and he has reason to be worried. Now he's going to need all the lucky shirts, and four-leaf clovers, and good-luck charms he can find.

Because when he turns the lock and pulls open Locker 13, Luke will actually be opening the door to . . . *THE NIGHTMARE ROOM.*

"Hey, Luke—good luck!"

Who called to me? The hall was jammed with kids excited about the first day of school. I was excited, too. My first day in seventh grade. My first day at Shawnee Valley Junior High.

I just *knew* this was going to be an awesome year.

Of course, I didn't take any chances. I wore my lucky shirt. It's a faded green T-shirt, kind of stretched out and the pocket is a little torn. But *no way* I'd start a school year without my lucky shirt.

And I had my lucky rabbit's foot in the pocket of my baggy khakis. It's black and very soft and furry. It's a key chain, but I don't want to ruin the good luck by hanging keys on it.

Why is it so lucky? Well, it's a *black* rabbit's foot, which is very rare. And I found it last November on my birthday. And after I found it, my parents gave me the new computer I wanted. So, it brought me good luck—right?

I glanced up at the red-and-black computer-printed

banner hanging over the hall: GO, SQUIRES! SUPPORT YOUR TEAM!

All of the boys' teams at Shawnee Valley are called the Squires. Don't ask me how they got that weird name. The banner made my heart race just a little. It reminded me that I had to find the basketball coach and ask when he was having tryouts.

I had a whole list of things I wanted to do: (1) check out the computer lab; (2) find out about the basketball team; (3) see if I could take any kind of special swimming program after school. I never went to a school with a swimming pool before. And since swimming is my other big sport, I was pretty pumped about it.

"Luke—hi!"

I spun around to find my friend Hannah Marcum behind me, looking as cheerful and enthusiastic as always. Hannah has short coppery hair, the color of a bright new penny, green eyes, and a great smile. My mother always calls her Sunshine, which totally embarrasses both of us.

"Your pocket is torn," she said. She tugged at it, ripping it a little more.

"Hey—get off!" I backed away. "It's my lucky shirt."

"Did you find your locker assignment yet?" She pointed to a group of kids studying a chart taped to the wall. They were all standing on tiptoe, trying to see over each other. "It's posted over there. Guess what? My locker is the first one outside the lunchroom. I'll be first for lunch every day."

"Oooh, lucky," I said.

"And I got Gruen for English," Hannah gushed. "He's the best! He's so funny. Everyone says you can't stop laughing. Did you get him too?"

"No," I said. "I got Warren."

Hannah made a face. "You're doomed."

"Shut up," I said. "Don't say things like that." I squeezed my rabbit's foot three times.

I pushed my way through the crowd to the locker chart. This is going to be an *excellent* year, I told myself. Junior High is *so* not like elementary school.

"Hey, man—how's it going?" Darnell Cross slapped me a high five.

"What's up?" I replied.

"Check it out. You got the *lucky* locker," Darnell said.

I squinted at the chart. "Huh? What do you mean?"

I ran my eyes down the list of names until I came to mine: Luke Greene. And then I followed the dotted line to my locker number.

And gasped.

"No way!" I said out loud. "That can't be right."

I blinked a few times, then focused on the chart again.

Yes. Locker 13.

Luke Greene . . . . #13

#13.

My breath caught in my throat. I started to choke.

I turned away from the chart, hoping no one could see how upset I was.

How can this be happening to me? I wondered. Locker 13? My whole year is *ruined* before it begins!

My heart pounded so hard, my chest ached. I forced myself to start breathing again.

I turned and found Hannah still standing there. "Where's your locker?" she asked. "I'll walk you there."

"Uh . . . well . . . I can deal with it," I said.

She squinted at me. "Excuse me?"

"I can deal with it," I repeated shakily. "It's Locker thirteen, but I can handle it. Really."

Hannah laughed. "Luke, you're such a superstitious geek!"

I frowned at her. "You mean that in a nice way—right?" I joked.

She laughed again and shoved me into a crowd of kids. I wish she wouldn't shove me so much. She's really strong.

I apologized to the kids I stumbled into. Then Hannah and I started down the crowded hall, checking the locker numbers, searching for number 13.

Just past the science lab, Hannah stopped suddenly and grabbed something up from the floor.

"Hey, wow! Look what I found!"

She held up a five-dollar bill. "Mmmmm—yes!"

She raised it to her lips and kissed it. "Five bucks! Yay!"

I sighed and shook my head. "Hannah, how come you're always so lucky?"

She didn't answer that question.

It seemed like a simple question, but it wasn't.

And if she had told me the answer, I think I would have run away—run as far as I could from Shawnee Valley Junior High, and never come back.

Let's skip ahead two months. . . .

Seventh grade was not bad so far. I made some new friends. I made real progress on the computer animation piece I had been working on for nearly two years. And I actually won a spot on the basketball team.

It was early November, about two weeks into the season. And I was late for practice.

Guys were already on the floor, doing stretching exercises, bouncing basketballs to each other, taking short layups. I crept to the locker room, hoping no one would notice me.

"Luke—get dressed. You're late!" Coach Bendix shouted.

I started to call, "Sorry. I got hung up in the computer lab." But that was no kind of excuse. So I just gave Coach a nod and started jogging full speed to the locker room to get changed.

My stomach felt kind of tight. I realized I wasn't looking forward to practice today. For a little guy, I'm a pretty good basketball player. I've got a good outside shot and pretty fast hands on defense.

I was so excited to make the team. But I wasn't counting on one problem—an eighth grader named Stretch Johannsen.

Stretch's real name is Shawn. But everyone in the world calls him Stretch—even his parents. You might wonder how he got that name. But if you saw him, you wouldn't wonder.

Stretch had some kind of a growth spurt last year in seventh grade, and he became a big blond giant practically overnight. He's taller than anyone in the high school. He has shoulders like a wrestler and long arms. I mean, *really* long arms, like a chimpanzee. He can reach halfway across the gym!

And that's why everyone started calling him Stretch.

I think a better name for him would be *Ostrich*. That's because he has long skinny legs, like bird legs, and a huge chest that's so wide it makes his pale, blue-eyed head look as tiny as an egg.

But I would never try my nickname on him. I don't think I can run fast enough. Stretch doesn't have much of a sense of humor. In fact, he's a pretty mean guy, always trash-talking and shoving people around—and not just on the basketball floor.

I think once he got over the shock of being a giant, he decided to be really impressed with himself.

Like being a giant is some kind of special talent or something.

But don't get me started. I'm always analyzing people, thinking too hard about them, about everything. Hannah is always telling me I think too much. But I don't get it. How do you stop thinking?

Last week after a practice, Coach Bendix said nearly the same thing. "You've got to play on instinct, Luke. There isn't time to think before every move."

Which, I guess, is another reason why I ride the bench. Of course, I'm only in seventh grade. So, unless another giant forward tries out for the Squires, I'll probably get to play next year—after Stretch graduates.

But for now, it's really embarrassing not to get to play. Especially since my parents come to every game to cheer me on. I sit on the team bench and watch Mom and Dad up in the gym bleachers, just staring at me. Staring . . .

It doesn't make you feel great.

Even the time-outs are painful. Stretch always comes trotting over to the team bench. He wipes the sweat off his face and body—and then throws the towel onto me. Like I'm some kind of towel boy!

During one time-out late in the first game, he took a long gulp of Gatorade and spit it onto my uniform shirt. I looked up and saw my parents watching from the bleachers.

Sad. Really sad . . .

Our team, the Squires, won our first two games, mainly because Stretch wouldn't let anyone else handle the ball. It was great to win—but I was already starting to feel like a loser. I wanted to play!

Maybe if I have a really strong practice today, Coach Bendix will try me out at guard, I told myself. Or maybe even as a backup center. I laced up my shoes and triple-knotted them for luck. Then I shut my eyes and counted to seven three times.

Just something I do.

I straightened my red-and-black uniform shorts, slammed the gym locker shut, and trotted out of the locker room and onto the floor. Guys were at the far end, taking three-point shots, everyone shooting at once. The balls bounced off each other, bounced off the hoop. The backboard rang out with a steady *thud thud thud*.

Some of the shots actually dropped in.

"Luke, get busy!" Coach yelled, motioning me to the basket. "Get some rebounds. Make some shots. Get loose!"

I flashed him a thumbs-up and ran to join the others. I saw Stretch leap up and make a high rebound. To my surprise, he spun around and heaved the ball at me. "Luke—think fast!"

I wasn't expecting it. The ball sailed through my

hands. I had to chase it to the wall. I dribbled back to find Stretch waiting. "Go ahead, man. Shoot."

I swallowed hard—and sent up a two-handed shot.

"He shoots—he *misses!*" Stretch shouted. Some guys laughed.

My shot bounced off the rim. Stretch took three fast strides, reached up his long arms, and grabbed the rebound in midair. He tossed it back to me. "Shoot again."

My next shot brushed the bottom of the net.

"He shoots—he *misses!*" Stretch repeated, as if that was the funniest thing anyone ever said. More loud laughter.

Stretch took the rebound and tossed me the ball. "Again," he ordered.

Everyone was watching now. I sent up a one-handed layup that almost dropped in. It rolled around the rim, then fell off.

"He shoots—he *misses!*"

I could feel sweat rolling down my forehead. Why can't I get lucky here? I asked myself. Come on, Luke—just one lucky shot. I slapped my left hand rapidly against the leg of my shorts seven times.

Stretch bounced the ball to me. "Go, champ. You're O for three. You got a streak going!" More laughter.

I shut my eyes for a second. Then I sailed this

one high—and gasped as it sank through the hoop.

Stretch grinned and shook his head. The other guys all cheered as if I'd just won the state junior high tournament.

I grabbed the ball and dribbled away from them. I didn't want to give Stretch a chance to ruin my victory. I knew he would keep me shooting till I was one for three hundred!

I turned to see if Coach Benson had watched my shot. He leaned against the wall, talking to two other teachers. He hadn't seen it.

I dribbled across the floor, then back toward the others. Then I made a big mistake.

A *really* big mistake. A mistake that ruined my life at Shawnee Valley Junior High.

"Hey, Stretch—think fast!" I shouted. And I heaved the ball at him as hard as I could.

What was I *thinking*?

I didn't see that he had bent down on one knee to tie his sneaker lace.

I froze in horror—and watched the ball fly at him. It hit him hard on the side of the head, knocked him over, and sent him tumbling to the floor.

"Hey—!" he cried out, stunned. He shook his head dizzily. I saw bright red blood start to flow from his nose.

"Stretch—I'm sorry!" I shrieked. "I didn't see you! I didn't mean—!"

I lurched forward, running to help him up.

"My contacts!" he cried. "You knocked out my contacts."

And then I heard a soft squish under my shoe.

I stopped. Lifted my foot. Stretch's contact lens lay flat as a pancake on the gym floor.

Everyone saw it.

Stretch was on his feet now. Blood rolled down his lips, his chin.

He didn't pay any attention to it. He had his eyes narrowed on me. He lumbered forward, clenching and unclenching his giant fists.

I was doomed.

Stretch reached under my arms and lifted me up. He was so huge and strong, he picked me off the floor like I was a ventriloquist's dummy.

"Whoa. It was an accident," I whispered.

"Here's *another* accident!" he said. When he talked, he spit blood in my face. He tightened his grip under my arms.

He raised me higher and gazed up at the basket. Is he going to make a three-point shot with me? I wondered.

Yes. He is. He's going to slam dunk me!

Behind me, I heard shouts. A whistle blowing. Running footsteps.

"Take it outside, Stretch!" I heard Coach Bendix shout.

Huh?

Stretch slowly lowered me to the floor. My knees started to buckle, but I managed to stay on my feet.

Stretch rubbed a hand across his bloody nose, then wiped it on the front of my jersey.

"Take it outside," Coach repeated, edging between us. "Let's pair up, everybody. One on one. Stretch—you and Luke."

"No way," Stretch muttered.

"He's your backup," Coach said, poking Stretch in the chest with his whistle. "You've got to teach Luke. I'm putting you in charge of Luke's development."

Stretch snickered. "Development? He doesn't have any development!"

"Go to my office. Get some tissues and stop that nosebleed," Coach instructed Stretch. "Then take Luke to the practice court behind the playground. Show him some moves. Teach him something."

Stretch stared at the floor for a few seconds, as if thinking it over. But he knew better than to argue with Coach Bendix. He nodded at me. "Let's go, Champ."

What choice did I have? Even though I knew it was pain time for me, I turned and followed him outside.

It was late afternoon, pretty cold to be outside in basketball shorts and a sleeveless jersey. Since it was November, the big, red sun had already lowered behind the houses across the street from the playground.

I shivered.

Stretch didn't give me much of a chance to get

ready. He pounded the ball hard on the asphalt court and came racing at me like a stampeding bull.

I tried to slide to the side. But Stretch lowered his shoulder and slammed it hard into my gut.

"Ohhh." I groaned and slumped back.

"Defense!" he shouted. "Get your hands up, Champ! Get ready. Here I come again!"

"No—wait—!" I pleaded.

The ball thundered in front of him as he drove into me again. This time he kept his body up straight. The force of the collision sent me sprawling to the asphalt.

"Defense!" he shouted. "Show me something. Block me. At least slow me down a little!"

Groaning again, I climbed to my feet. I felt as if I'd been hit by a truck.

Stretch dribbled around me, circling me, his eyes locked angrily on me. His nosebleed had stopped, but he still had dried blood caked under his nose.

I rubbed my chest. "I . . . I think I broke a rib," I whispered.

With a wild shout, he slammed into me again. This time I flew back—and smashed into the thick wooden post that held up the backboard.

"You're going to pay for those contacts, Champ," he called, hulking over me so I couldn't stand up, dribbling the ball inches from my feet.

"Yeah. Okay," I said, trying to rub the pain from my chest. "I said I was sorry."

"You're gonna be more sorry," he said. He bounced the ball hard against my bare leg. "Get up."

I didn't move. "It was an accident," I insisted. "I really didn't see you bend down. Really."

He picked at the caked blood under his nose. "Get up. Let's go. I'm supposed to teach you something." He laughed really loud. I'm not sure why. Then he swept a huge hand back through his short white-blond hair and waited for me to stand up. So he could teach me more lessons.

I climbed shakily to my feet. I felt so dizzy, I had to grab the wooden post. My head ached. My ribs ached.

"Can we . . . uh . . . play a different game?" I asked weakly.

"Yeah. Sure," he said. "Hey—think fast!"

He was standing so close, and he heaved the ball so hard, it felt like a cannonball as it shot into my stomach.

I stumbled back. And let out a sharp gasp.

And then realized I couldn't breathe.

I struggled hard to suck in some air.

No . . . no air . . . I . . . can't . . . get . . . air. . . .

I saw bright yellow stars. The yellow darkened to red.

Pain shot through my chest. The pain spread, growing sharper, sharper.

I was down on my back now, staring up at the

sky, staring up at the dancing red stars. I wanted to scream. But I had no air.

Can't breathe . . . can't breathe at all. . . .

The stars faded away. The color faded from the sky.

All black. All black now.

And as I sank into the blackness, I heard a voice.

A beautiful, soft voice from far, far away. Calling my name.

An angel, I realized.

Yes. Through the blackness, I heard an angel calling my name.

And I knew that I had died.

"Luke? Luke?"

The blackness lifted. I blinked up at the afternoon sky. The voice was closer now. And I recognized it.

"Luke?"

My chest ached as I took a deep breath.

Hey—when had I started to breathe again?

I lifted my head and saw Hannah running across the basketball court. She wore a blue windbreaker, unzipped, and it flapped up over her shoulders like wings. Her red hair glowed in the late afternoon sun like a halo.

Not an angel. Just Hannah.

She turned angrily to Stretch as she ran past him. "What did you do to Luke—*kill* him?"

Stretch giggled. "Probably."

Hannah dropped onto her knees beside me. Her windbreaker fell over my face. She tugged it away. "Are you alive? Can you speak?"

"Yeah. I'm okay," I muttered. I felt like a jerk. A helpless jerk.

Stretch walked up behind Hannah. "Who's she?" he sneered at me. "Your *girlfriend*?"

Hannah spun around to face him. "Hey—I've seen *your* girlfriend!"

Stretch's mouth dropped open. "Huh? Who's that?"

"Godzilla!" Hannah declared.

I tried to laugh, but it made my ribs hurt.

The next thing I knew, Hannah was on her feet, shoving Stretch's shoulders with both hands, forcing him to back up. "Ever hear of picking on someone your own size?" she demanded.

Stretch laughed. "No. Tell me about it." He backed away from her and raised his big, meaty fists. He grinned and started dancing like a fighter. "Come on. You want a piece of me? You want a piece of me?" Imitating someone in a movie, I guess.

"One on one," Hannah challenged.

Stretch tossed back his head and laughed. His blue eyes rolled around in his tiny head. "You want a piece of me?"

"Freestyle shooting," Hannah said, tearing off the windbreaker. She tossed it to the side of the court. "Come on, Stretch. Twenty shots each. Any kind of shot." She stared up at him. "You'll lose. Really. You'll see. You'll lose to a *girl*!"

His smile faded. "You're on the girls' basketball team—right?"

Hannah nodded. "I'm the center."

Stretch started to dribble the ball slowly in front of him. "Twenty shots? Layups or three-point?"

Hannah shrugged. "Any kind. You'll lose."

I climbed to my feet and went over to the side of the court to watch. I still felt a little shaky, but I knew I was okay.

Stretch didn't hesitate. He raised the ball and pushed up a one-handed shot from half-court. The ball hit the backboard, then the rim—and dropped in. "One for one," he said. He ran to retrieve the ball. "I'll keep shooting until I miss."

He missed his next shot, an easy layup from under the basket.

Hannah's turn. I crossed my fingers and counted to seven three times.

"Go, Hannah!" I cheered, holding up my crossed fingers.

Hannah sank a basket from the foul line. Then she drove under the basket and shot another one in from underneath.

My mouth dropped open as she sank eight more baskets without a miss. "Wow. Go, Hannah!"

Stretch just stood there looking dumb. I couldn't tell what he was thinking. His face was a total blank.

"Ten for ten!" Hannah declared. She bounced the ball to Stretch. "You go. Just to keep it interesting."

Hannah glanced at me, grinned, and flashed me a thumbs-up.

Stretch wasn't smiling anymore. He had a grim,

determined look on his face as he drove in close to shoot. He dropped four straight baskets, then missed one from in front of the foul line.

He muttered something under his breath and bounced the ball to Hannah.

Hannah sank eight more in a row. She turned to Stretch. "Eighteen for eighteen!"

But he was already jogging back to the gym, a scowl on his face.

"I'm not finished!" Hannah called after him.

Stretch turned back to me. "Hey, Champ—maybe you should take a lesson from your *girlfriend*. Or maybe you should play on her team!" Shaking his head, he disappeared into the school.

A strong wind began to blow across the playground. It was dark as evening now. I picked up Hannah's windbreaker and reached out to hand it to her. But she took another shot. "Nineteen." And then another. "Twenty. Yay! I win!"

I gaped at her. "Hannah—you never miss! How do you *do* that?"

She shrugged. "Just lucky."

I shivered. We started jogging back to the school. "Ask me how lucky I am," I muttered. "I made a new enemy today. A *huge* enemy!"

Hannah stopped and grabbed my arm. "Hey—I totally forgot why I was looking for you. I wanted to tell you the coolest news!"

I held the school door open. "Yeah? What?"

Hannah's green eyes flashed. "You know those photos I took of my dog? I sent them to a magazine in New York. And guess what? They paid me *five hundred dollars* for them. They're going to publish them—and do a big story about me! Isn't that so totally cool?"

"Wow. Totally," I said.

And that's when I decided my luck had to change.

Why should Hannah have all the luck? I can be lucky, too, I told myself.

It's all attitude. That's what it takes. The right attitude.

I changed into my street clothes. I made my way upstairs to stop at my locker. Locker 13.

Basketball practice had run so late, the halls were empty. My shoes clonked noisily on the hard floor. Most of the lights had already been turned off.

This school is creepy when it's empty, I decided. I stopped in front of my locker, feeling a chill at the back of my neck.

I always felt a little weirded-out in front of the locker. For one thing, it wasn't with all the other seventh-grade lockers. It was down at the end of the back hall, by itself, just past a janitor's supply closet.

Up and down the hall, all the other lockers had been painted over the summer. They were all a smooth, silvery gray. But no one had touched locker 13. The old, green paint was peeling and had large patches scraped off. Deep scratches crisscrossed up and down the door.

The locker smelled damp. And sour. As if it had once been filled with rotting leaves or dead fish or something.

That's okay, I can deal with this, I told myself.

I took a deep breath. New attitude, Luke. New attitude. Your luck is going to change.

I opened my backpack and pulled out a fat, black marker. Then I closed the locker door. And right above the number 13, I wrote the word LUCKY in big, bold capital letters.

I stepped back to admire my work: LUCKY 13.

"Yessss!" I felt better already.

I shoved the black marker into my backpack and started to zip it up. And that's when I heard the breathing.

Soft, soft breaths. So soft, I thought I imagined them. From inside the locker?

I crept closer and pressed my ear against the door.

I heard a soft hiss. Then more breathing.

The backpack slipped out of my hands and thudded to the floor. I froze.

And heard another soft hiss inside the locker. It ended in a short cry.

The back of my neck prickled. My breath caught in my throat.

Without realizing it, my hand had gripped the locker handle.

Should I open the door? Should I?

My hand tightened on the handle. I forced myself to start breathing again.

I'm imagining this, I told myself.

There can't be anyone breathing inside my locker.

I lifted the handle. Pulled open the door.

"Hey—!" I cried out in shock. And stared down at a black cat.

The cat gazed up at me, its eyes red in the dim hall light. The black fur stood up on its back. It pulled back its lips and hissed again.

A black cat?

A black cat inside my locker?

I'm imagining this, I thought.

I blinked hard, trying to blink the cat away.

A black cat inside locker 13? Could there be any *worse* luck?

"How—how did you get in there?" I choked out.

The cat hissed again and arched its back. It gazed up at me coldly.

Then it leaped from the locker floor. It darted over

my shoes, down the hall. Running rapidly, silently. Head down, tail straight up, it turned the first corner and disappeared.

I stared after it, my heart pounding. I could still feel its furry body brushing against my leg. I realized I was still gripping the locker handle.

My head spun with questions. How long had the cat been in there? How did it get inside the locked door? Why was there a black cat in my locker? Why?

I turned and checked out the floor of the locker. Just to make sure there weren't any other creatures hiding in there. Then, still feeling confused, I closed the door carefully, locked it, and stepped back.

LUCKY 13.

The black letters appeared to glow.

"Yeah. Lucky," I muttered, picking up my backpack. "Real lucky. A black cat in my locker."

I held my lucky rabbit's foot and kept squeezing it tightly all the way home.

Things are going to change, I told myself. Things have got to change. . . .

But in the next few weeks my luck didn't change at all.

One day after school I was on my way to the computer lab when I ran into Hannah. "Where are you going?" she asked. "Want to come watch my basketball game?"

"I can't," I replied. "I promised to install some

new modems for Mrs. Coffey, the computer teacher."

"Mr. Computer Geek strikes again!" she said. She started jogging toward the gym.

"Did you get your science test back?" I called after her.

She stopped and turned around with a grin on her face. "You won't believe it, Luke. I didn't have time to study. I had to guess on every question. And guess what? I got a hundred! I got them all right!"

"That's excellent!" I called. I'd studied for that test for a solid week, and I got a seventy-four.

I made my way into the computer lab and waved to Mrs. Coffey. She was hunched over her desk, sorting through a tall stack of disks. "Hey, how's it going?" she called.

The computer lab is my second home. Ever since Mrs. Coffey learned that I can repair computers, and upgrade them, and install things in them, I've been her favorite student.

And I have to admit, I really like her too. Whenever I don't have basketball practice, I check in at the computer lab to talk with her and see what needs to be fixed.

"Luke, how is your animation project coming along?" she asked, setting down the disks. She brushed back her blond hair. She has the nicest smile. Everyone likes her because she always seems to enjoy her classes so much.

"I'm almost ready to show it to you," I said. I sat

down in front of a computer and started to remove the back. "I think it's really cool. And it's going much faster now. I found a new way to move pixels around."

Her eyes grew wide. "Really?"

"It's a very cool invention," I said, carefully sliding the insides from the computer. "The program is pretty simple. I think a lot of animators might like it."

I set down my screwdriver and gazed across the room at her. "Maybe you could help me. You know. Show it to people. Get it copyrighted or something."

"Maybe," she said. She stood up, smoothing the hem of her blue sweater over her jeans. She came up behind me and watched as I removed the old modem. "You're really skillful, Luke. I think you're going to make a lot of money with computers some day."

"Yeah. Maybe," I replied awkwardly. "Thanks." I didn't really know what to say. Mrs. Coffey is so awesome. She is the only teacher who really encourages me and thinks I'm somebody.

"I can't *wait* to show you my animation," I said.

"Well . . . I have some big news," she said suddenly. I turned and caught the excited smile on her face. "You're the first person to hear it, Luke. Can you keep a secret?"

"Yeah. Okay," I said.

"I just got the most wonderful job! At a really big software company in Chicago. I'm leaving school next week!"

• • •

The next afternoon I couldn't check in at the computer lab. I had to hurry to the swimming pool behind the gym.

Swimming is my other big sport. I spent all last summer working with an instructor at our local pool. He was fast enough to make the Olympic tryouts a few years ago. And he really improved my stroke and showed me a lot of secrets for getting my speed up.

So I looked forward to the tryouts for the Squires swim team. I couldn't wear my lucky swimsuit because it didn't fit anymore. But I wore my lucky shirt to school that day. And as I changed for the pool, I silently counted to seven three times.

As I left the locker room, I heard shouts and laughter echoing off the tile pool walls. Feeling my heart start to race, I stepped into the steamy air of the indoor pool. The floor was puddled with warm water. I inhaled the sharp chlorine smell. I love that smell!

Then I bent down and kissed the top of the diving board. I know. It sounds weird. But it's just something I always do.

I turned to the pool. Three or four guys were already in the water. At the shallow end I saw Stretch. He was violently splashing two other guys. He had them cornered at the end of the pool. His big hands slapped the water, sending up tall waves over them. They pleaded with him to give them a break.

Coach Swanson blew his whistle, then shouted

for Stretch to cut the horseplay. Stretch gave the two guys one more vicious splash.

Then he turned and saw me. "Hey, Champ—" he shouted, his voice booming off the tiles. "You're early. Drowning lessons are next week! Ha ha! Nice swim trunks. Are those your *girlfriend's*? Ha ha!"

A few other guys laughed too.

I decided to ignore them. I was feeling pretty confident. About twenty guys were trying out. I knew there were only six spots open on the team. But after all my work last summer, I thought I could make the top six.

We all warmed up for a bit, taking easy laps, limbering up our muscles, getting used to the warm water. After a few minutes, Coach Swanson made us all climb out and line up at the deep end of the pool.

"Okay, guys, I've got to get to my night job by five, so we're going to keep this simple," the coach announced. "You have one chance. One chance only. You hear the whistle, you do a speed dive into the pool. You do two complete laps, any stroke you want. I'll take the first six guys. And two alternates. Any questions?"

There weren't any.

Everyone leaned forward, preparing to dive. Stretch lined up next to me. He elbowed me hard in the side. "Give me some room, Champ. Don't crowd me."

Okay, so he'll come in first, I figured, rubbing the pain from my side. That leaves five other places on the team.

I'm good enough, I told myself. I know I am. I know I am. . . .

The whistle blew. All down the row, bodies tensed, then plunged forward.

I started my dive—and slipped.

The pool floor—so wet . . .

My feet slid on the tile.

Oh . . . no!

I hit the water with a loud *smack*.

A belly flop! No kind of dive.

Struggling to recover, I raised my head. And saw everyone way ahead of me.

One unlucky slip . . .

I lowered my head, determined to catch up. I started stroking easily, forcing myself to be calm. I remembered the slow, steady, straight-legged kick my instructor had taught me.

I sped up. I passed some guys. Hit the wall and started back.

I can do this, I told myself. I can still make the team.

Faster . . .

At the end of the second lap the finish was a furious blur. Blue water. Thrashing arms and legs. Loud breaths. Bobbing heads.

I tried to shut out everything and concentrate on

my stroke . . . ignore everyone else . . . and swim!

At last my hand hit the pool wall. I ducked under, then surfaced, blowing out water. I wiped my hair away from my eyes. The taste of chlorine was in my mouth. Water running down my face, I glanced around.

I didn't finish last. Some guys were still swimming. I squinted down the line of swimmers who had finished. How many? How many were ahead of me?

"Luke—you're seventh," Coach Swanson announced. He made a large check on his clipboard. "First alternate. See you at practice."

I was still too out-of-breath to reply.

Seventh.

I let out a long sigh. I felt so disappointed. I could do better than seventh, I knew. If only I hadn't slipped.

As I started to trudge back to the locker room, Stretch strode up beside me. "Hey, Champ!" He slapped my bare back with his open hand, so hard it made a loud *smack*. "Thanks for making me look so good!"

I got dressed quickly, standing in a corner by myself. A few guys came over to say congratulations. But I didn't feel I deserved it.

Across the locker room Stretch was still in his swim trunks. He was having a great time, smacking guys with his towel, really making the towel *snap* against their bare skin, laughing his head off.

I tossed my towel in the basket. Then I stepped up to the mirror over the sinks to comb my hair. A ceiling lightbulb was out, and I had to lean over the sink to see.

I had just started to comb my wet hair back—when I saw the jagged crack along the length of the glass.

"Whoa." I stopped combing and stepped back.

A broken mirror. Seven years bad luck for someone.

I reached into my khakis pocket and squeezed my rabbit's foot three times. Then I turned back to the mirror and began combing my hair again.

Something was wrong.

I blinked. Once. Twice.

A red light? Some kind of red glare in the mirror glass.

I squinted into the glass—and let out a cry.

The red glare was coming from a pair of eyes—two red eyes, glowing like hot coals.

Two angry red eyes, floating in the glass. Floating beside my reflection.

I could see my confused expression as I stared at the frightening red eyes . . . as I watched the eyes slide across the glass . . . slide . . . slide closer . . . until their red glow covered my eyes!

My horrified reflection stared out at me with the fiery, glowing eyes.

And I opened my mouth and let out a long, terrified scream.

Over my scream I heard heavy footsteps behind me. And then I heard a voice—Stretch's voice: "Hey—get used to it!"

I spun around. He grinned at me. "Get used to it, Champ. That's your face! It makes other people scream too!"

"No!" I cried. "No! It's not! Don't you see—?"

Coach Swanson burst in behind Stretch. "Luke—what's wrong?"

"My eyes!" I cried. "Look! Are they red? *Are* they?"

Coach Swanson and Stretch exchanged glances.

"What is his problem?" Stretch murmured.

Coach Swanson stepped up close and examined my eyes. "What's wrong with you, Luke? It's just the chlorine from the pool. Your eyes will be okay in a little while."

"Chlorine? Huh? No!" I insisted. Then I glanced into the mirror. And saw my normal, brown eyes gazing back at me.

No glowing eyes. No red eyes burning in the glass like an evil movie monster.

"Uh . . . well . . ." I rubbed my eyes. They didn't burn or anything. They felt okay.

I turned back to Stretch and Coach Swanson. I didn't know what to say to them. They were both still staring at me as if I were nuts.

And maybe I was.

Black cats jumping out of my locker? Glowing red eyes in the mirror?

"Well . . . see you at practice," I said.

Stretch laughed. "Not if I see you first! Ha ha!"

I laughed too. It wasn't funny, but I wanted to sound calm again, normal.

As I followed them out of the locker room, I realized I was trembling.

Why were these strange things happening to me?

After dinner I was supposed to go to the mall with Hannah. She wanted to buy me some computer software for my birthday. But she wanted me to pick it out.

That was really nice of her. But at the last minute I decided not to go.

I was still feeling weird from the swim tryouts. And I wanted to work on my animation project. If I worked really hard, I might be able to get it finished in time to show Mrs. Coffey before she left school.

I went up to my room and booted up the animation. But I couldn't concentrate. I kept staring at the four-leaf clover inside a block of clear Lucite I keep on my desk. And I kept jumping up and running to the mirror to check my eyes.

Perfectly normal.

Not glowing.

So what happened? What happened to me in that locker room? I asked myself. I tried to convince myself there was something wrong with the mirror.

The red glow was because of the way the light hit the crack in the mirror. Or something.

No.

That didn't make sense.

The phone rang a little before ten o'clock. And it was Hannah, sounding very breathless and excited.

"Luke—you should've come! You should've come!"

I had to hold the phone away from my ear, Hannah was shouting so loud. "Why? What happened?" I asked.

"I won it!" she declared. "Do you believe it? I won!"

"Excuse me? Hannah—what are you talking about?"

"You know the raffle at the mall? That huge red SUV? It's been on display there for a month? Thousands of people put tickets in the box. Thousands! And—and—I just happened to be walking by when they had the drawing tonight. And—"

"You *didn't*!" I shrieked.

"Yes! Yes! I won it! I won the SUV!"

"Wow!" I slumped onto my bed. I actually felt faint. My heart was pounding as if I had won!

"You should've seen me when they called out my name!" Hannah gushed. "I screamed. I just stood there and screamed!"

She screamed again, shrieked at the top of her lungs. A long, high, joyful scream.

"Hannah—that's so awesome," I said. I don't think she heard me. She was still screaming.

"My family is so happy, Luke. You should *see* them. They are *dancing* around the living room!"

"That's so great," I said.

Hannah lowered her voice. "I just feel bad about one thing, Luke. I was so crazed, I was so *berserk,* I forgot why I was at the mall. I forgot all about buying you a birthday gift."

I stood up. I picked up the block with the four-leaf clover inside and smoothed it between my hands. "That's okay," I told Hannah. "I just decided what I really want for my birthday."

"What's that?" she asked.

"I want *your* luck!"

Hannah laughed. She thought I was kidding. But of course I was serious.

"Are you going to school tomorrow?" she asked.

"Huh? Yeah, sure. Why not?"

"Tomorrow is Friday the thirteenth," she said. "I know how superstitious you are. I thought maybe you'd stay home and hide under the bed all day."

"Ha ha," I said. But I felt a cold tingle at the back of my neck. "I'll be there," I told Hannah. "I'm not totally wacko, you know."

But I'll wear my lucky shirt, I thought. And I'll take my four-leaf clover in my backpack. And I'll ask Mom to pack my lucky sandwich for lunch—peanut butter and mayonnaise.

"I have to go to school tomorrow," I told Hannah. "I have basketball practice after school."

"How's practice going?" Hannah asked.

I chuckled. "Not bad. So far, I haven't gotten any splinters from sitting on the bench!"

Hannah laughed. I could hear shouts and wild laughter in the background. "I've got to go!" she said, shouting over the racket. "My family is still celebrating my winning the SUV! Bye!"

She clicked off before I could reply.

That night I dreamed about locker 13.

In the dream I stepped up to the locker. Someone had taped a calendar to the door. I came closer and saw that Friday the thirteenth had been circled in red.

I started to rip the calendar off the locker door. But I stopped when I heard loud breathing. Hoarse wheezing sounds. Like someone was having trouble breathing.

I touched the locker door. And it was burning hot!

I screamed in shock and pulled my hand away.

Again, I heard the hoarse breathing from inside the locker. And then I heard a tiny voice cry out: *"Please . . . get me out."*

In the dream I knew I was dreaming. I wanted to lift myself out of the dream. But I was stuck there. And I knew I had no choice. I had to pull open the locker door and see who was in there.

"*Please . . . I want out. Get me out!*" the tiny, frightened voice called.

Even though I knew I was dreaming, I still felt so frightened. Real fear that makes you shake, whether you're awake or asleep.

I watched myself grip the door handle. Slowly—so slowly—I pulled the locker door open.

And I stared in horror at the figure huddled inside the locker. *Because it was ME!*

It was me inside the locker, hugging myself, trembling all over. It was me—and my eyes started to glow. My eyes glowed out from the dark locker, red as fire.

And as I stared at myself, stared at those ugly, evil red eyes, I watched my face begin to change. I watched hair grow out of my nostrils. Long braids of thick black hair, sliding out of my nose—down, down to the locker floor.

Beneath the shining red eyes, thick, black, twisted ropes of hair were pouring from my nose. Out of the locker. Piling onto the hall floor. Curling around me as I watched.

Yes. The long hair flowed from my nose and snaked around me as I watched in horror. Curled around me, covering me in warm, scratchy hair. Covering me like a big, furry coat, and then tightening. Tightening. Tightening around my chest. Tightening around my face. Wrapping me like a mummy. Wrapping me in my ghastly nose hair.

I woke up, one hand tightly wrapped around the Lucite block with the four-leaf clover. Gray morning sunlight seeped through my bedroom window. My room was so cold, cold as a freezer.

"Luke, what are you doing up there? You're late!" Mom's voice shattered the frozen silence.

"A dream," I murmured. A hoarse laugh escaped my throat. My eyes darted around the room. Normal. Everything normal.

"Hurry, Luke! It's really late." Mom's voice sounded so good to me.

I followed her order. I hurried. I got showered, dressed, ate breakfast, and arrived at school with about two minutes to spare. The halls were pretty empty. Most kids had already gone to their homerooms.

I glanced at the clock on the tile wall. Then jogged to the end of the back hall to toss my jacket into my locker.

But a few feet from my locker I stopped with a gasp.

What was that on the door to locker 13?

I crept closer.

A calendar?

Yes.

Someone had taped a calendar to the door. And . . . and today . . . Friday the thirteenth was circled in red.

"My dream!" I murmured.

That horrifying dream. It's coming true, I realized. I'm going to open the door, and it's going to come true.

I stared at the calendar, at the number 13 circled in red marker.

Last night's dream played itself again through my mind. I shuddered. My legs and arms itched. I could practically feel the disgusting hair curling around my skin.

With an angry cry I ripped the calendar off the door and crumpled it in my hand.

Now I expected to hear the heavy breathing from inside the locker. And the tiny cries—my cries—begging to be let out.

But I didn't wait. "I'm not opening it," I said out loud.

No way am I going to allow the dream to come true.

I tossed the wadded-up calendar sheet to the floor. Then I spun around and began running to class. The hall was empty. My shoes thudded loudly on the hard floor as I ran.

I'll keep my coat with me, I decided. I'll just drag

it around with me all day. I don't need to open the locker.

The bell rang as I reached my homeroom door. Mr. Perkins looked up as I burst into the room. "Good morning, Luke," he said. "Running a little late this morning?"

"A little," I replied breathlessly. Unzipping my jacket, I started to my seat.

"Would you like time to go hang your coat in your locker?" Mr. Perkins asked.

"Uh . . . no. That's okay." I lowered my backpack to the floor and dropped into the chair. "I'll just . . . keep it."

A few kids were staring at me. Mr. Perkins nodded and turned back to the papers he was reading.

I took a deep breath and settled back against the chair. I rubbed the right sleeve of my lucky shirt seven times.

That dream is *not* going to come true! I told myself. No way! I won't let it.

Of course, I wasn't thinking clearly. How *could* that crazy dream come true?

If I had stopped for one second to think about it, I would have realized the whole idea was insane.

But today was Friday the thirteenth. And I *never* can think clearly on Friday the thirteenth. I admit it. I'm always a little crazy on that unlucky day.

I glanced up to see that Mr. Perkins had been reading the morning announcements. I hadn't heard a word he said. I pulled the four-leaf clover from my backpack, twirled it in my hand, and wished for good luck for the rest of the day.

At noon I found Hannah at a table against the back wall of the lunchroom. She was sitting all by herself, staring down at her brown lunchbag, which she hadn't opened.

"Hi. Whassup?" I dropped across from her.

"Hi," she said softly, without raising her eyes. "How's it going?"

"Well, pretty okay for a Friday the thirteenth," I said. Actually, the morning had flown by without any problems at all.

I expected Hannah to make some kind of joke about how superstitious I am. But she didn't say a word.

I pulled the sandwich from my bag and started to unwrap the foil. "My lucky sandwich," I said. "Peanut butter and mayonnaise."

"Yum," she said, rolling her eyes. She finally looked at me. She appeared tired. Her eyes were bloodshot, red, as if she'd been crying. Her hair was a mess, and her face was gray.

"How come you're wearing your coat?" she asked.

"Oh . . . uh . . . no reason," I said. "I was kind of cold."

She nodded glumly.

"Did you come to school in the new SUV?" I asked.

She shook her head. "We don't have it yet. Dad has to go fill out a lot of papers." She let out a long sigh.

I lowered my sandwich. "Are you feeling okay?" I asked.

She didn't answer. Instead, she sighed again and stared down at the table.

I poked her lunchbag with one finger. "What do you have for lunch?"

She shrugged. "Just some fruit. I'm not very hungry." She opened the bag, reached a hand in, and pulled out a bright yellow banana.

She struggled with the skin. Then finally peeled it open.

"Oh, yuck!" Her face twisted in disgust. She dropped the banana to the table.

Inside the skin, the banana was completely rotten. Just a soft pile of black mush. A horrible, sour smell—like ripe vomit—floated up from it.

Hannah shoved the banana away. "Sick. That's really sick."

"The skin is perfectly fresh," I said. "How could the banana be so rotten?"

"I think I have an apple," Hannah said glumly. She tore the bag apart and pulled out a red apple. She twirled it between her hands—then stopped with a gasp.

I saw the deep, dark hole on the side of the apple. And as we both stared at it, a fat, brown worm—at least two inches long—curled out from inside. And then another. And another.

The worms dropped from the apple, onto the tabletop.

"I don't *believe* this!" Hannah shrieked. She scraped her chair back so hard, it toppled over.

And before I could say anything, she was running from the room.

After school I looked for Hannah on my way to basketball practice. I was worried about her. She had acted so weird at lunch. Not like herself at all.

I reminded myself that it was Friday the thirteenth. And sometimes people act a little weird on this day.

But not Hannah. Hannah is the least superstitious person I know. She walks under ladders all the time, and she hugs black cats, and doesn't think a thing of it.

And why should she? Hannah has to be the luckiest person on earth!

Lockers slammed as kids prepared to go home. I started to the gym, then turned back. I don't want to carry my coat and backpack to the gym, I decided. I'm going to stuff them in my locker.

I hesitated as the locker came into view at the end of the hall. I read the words on the door: LUCKY 13. Of course I remembered my nightmare—and the calendar from my nightmare taped on the locker door.

But I had to open the locker. I didn't want to carry my stuff around with me for the rest of the year!

"Hey, Luke!" I saw Darnell Cross waving to me from the doorway to the science lab. "Are the Squires going to beat Davenport?"

"They're not so tough," I called back. "We could take them."

"You going to play?" Darnell asked. He grinned because he already knew the answer.

"As soon as I grow taller than Stretch!" I replied.

He laughed and disappeared back into the lab.

I stepped up to locker 13. I brought my face close to the door. "Anyone in there?" I called in.

Silence.

"Just checking," I said. I grabbed the door handle. I was feeling pretty confident. Friday the thirteenth was two-thirds over, and so far, nothing terribly unlucky had happened to me.

I squeezed my rabbit's foot for luck. Then I took a deep breath—and pulled open the locker.

Nothing unusual inside the locker.

I realized I was still gripping the rabbit's foot inside my pocket. I let go of it and slipped my backpack off my shoulders.

I studied the locker carefully. A bunch of books and notebooks on the top shelf, where I had left them. My old gray sweatshirt lay crumpled on the locker floor.

No black cats. No one breathing or crying or shooting piles of hair from his nose.

I let out a long sigh of relief. Then I tossed the backpack on top of the balled-up sweatshirt. Shoved my jacket onto the hook on the back wall.

I started to slam the door shut when I spotted something at my feet.

My shoe kicked it and it rolled against the locker bottom, then bounced back.

A ball?

I bent down and picked it up. I raised it close to my face.

"Whoa." Not a ball. A tiny yellow skull, a little larger than a Ping-Pong ball.

It had an open-mouthed grin, revealing two rows of gray teeth. I ran my finger over the teeth. They were hard and bumpy.

I squeezed it. The little skull was made of some kind of hard rubber.

The eyes—sunken deep in the sockets—were red glass. They glowed in the hall lights, like tiny rubies.

"Where did you come from?" I asked it.

I turned back to the locker. Did the skull fall out of the locker? How did it get in there? Was someone playing some kind of Friday the thirteenth head game with me?

I decided that had to be the answer.

I rolled the skull around in my hand a few times. I poked my finger against the glowing, red glass eyes.

Then I tucked it into my pants pocket. I slammed the locker shut—and headed to practice.

"Look alive! Heads up. Look alive!" Coach Bendix was shouting.

I ran out of the locker room and grabbed a basketball off the ball rack. I began dribbling around the floor.

We were having one of Coach's free-for-all practices. That meant we had to keep moving, keep playing—run, dribble, pass, shoot, play defense. Do everything all at once in a big free-for-all.

I dribbled slowly across the floor, concentrating hard. Trying not to lose the dribble. I saw Stretch turn toward me. He stuck out both hands and moved forward, ready to block me.

I decided to try and fake him out. I dribbled left—and moved right. I edged past him easily. Moved under the basket. And sent up a shot that sailed across the gym and dropped in.

"Hey—one for one!" I cried happily.

"Lucky shot!" Stretch called.

I took the ball and moved back to the top of the key. I sent up a two-handed jumpshot. It soared over the rim—and dropped through the basket with a soft *swish*.

"Yes!" I pumped my fists in the air.

I didn't have long to celebrate. I turned and saw Stretch barreling toward me, dribbling hard, leaning forward with grim determination.

He's going to charge right over me, I realized. He's going to *flatten* me.

Guys backed out of his way as Stretch flew across the floor.

"Look out, Luke!" someone shouted.

I froze for a moment. Then I ducked to the left. Stuck out my hand and slapped the ball away from Stretch.

He made a wild grab for it. But I dribbled it out of

his reach. Then I spun around and sent a wild, high shot into the air. The ball hit the glass backboard—and sank through the net.

"Wow!"

"Way to go, Luke!"

"Three for three!"

The other players were in shock.

Stretch shook his head. "Feeling lucky, today? Think fast!" He pulled back his long arm—and heaved the ball at my chest with all his strength.

I caught it easily. Dribbled it three times. Shot—and dropped another basket.

Stretch scowled. "I don't believe this," he muttered, shaking his head.

I don't, either! I thought to myself. I've never shot four baskets in a row in my life!

I turned and saw Coach Bendix watching me. Was this my big chance? Stretch and another player were passing the ball back and forth, moving across the floor.

I shot forward. Intercepted Stretch's pass. Drove to the basket. And sent up an easy layup. "Two points!" I cried.

With an angry grunt Stretch reached for the rebound. But I pushed it out of his hands. Grabbed it. Spun. Shot again. "Two points!"

Stretch cried out angrily. He bumped me hard

from behind. I think he would have flattened me on the spot. But he saw that Coach Bendix was running over to us.

Coach slapped me on the back. "Way to go, Luke!" he boomed. "Way to show real improvement! I'm impressed. Keep it up, okay? I'm going to give you some playing time next Friday."

"Hey—thanks," I replied breathlessly.

I saw Stretch scowl. Saw his face turn an angry red.

I grabbed a ball and dribbled away. I wanted to shout and jump for joy. Had my luck finally changed?

It seemed that way. Suddenly I could pass and jump and shoot and play defense like I never could before! It was as if I was possessed or something! Possessed by an all-star athlete.

In the locker room after practice, Stretch ignored me. But other guys slapped me on the back and flashed me a thumbs-up.

"Lookin' good, Luke!"

"Way to go, man!"

"Go, Squires!"

I was feeling really happy. Like a new person. As I changed into my street clothes, I felt the little skull in my pants pocket. I pulled it out and gazed at it, smoothing my thumb over the hard rubber.

"Are you my new good-luck charm?" I asked it.

The tiny, red eyes glowed back at me. I kissed it, gave it a smack on top of its yellow head, and shoved it back into my pants pocket.

That skull is going everywhere with me, I decided. It's got to be lucky.

It's *got* to be!

As I walked home, I kept reliving my great basketball triumph. I pictured my long, perfect jump-shots again. And I saw myself stealing the ball from Stretch's hands, driving right past him, and scoring. Embarrassing him. Embarrassing Stretch again and again!

Wow! What a day!

It was a cold, gray afternoon. Dark clouds hung low over the nearly bare trees. It felt more like winter than fall.

A few blocks from home, I crossed a street—and heard a short cry.

A long, low evergreen hedge ran across the front yard on the corner. I stopped, gazing over the hedge. Had the cry come from the yard?

I listened hard. Down the block a car door slammed. A dog started to bark. The wind made a whistling sound through the phone lines overhead.

And then I heard it—another sharp cry—longer this time.

A baby? It sounded like a baby's cry.

"Owwwww. Owwwwww."

I lowered my gaze to the hedge—and saw the creature making the shrill cries.

A cat. No. A small orange-and-white kitten.

It appeared to be stuck in the prickly brambles of the hedge.

"Owwwww. Owwwwww."

Carefully I bent down and gently lifted the cat out with both hands. As I cupped my hands around it, it stopped crying immediately. But it was still breathing hard, its white chest moving rapidly up and down. I rubbed its head, trying to soothe it.

"You're okay, little kitten," I whispered.

And then I heard another cry. A loud shriek.

I looked up to see a large woman running at me angrily. Her face was bright red, and she waved her arms furiously.

"Oh, no," I muttered. I nearly dropped the cat.

Why is she so angry?

What have I done?

"The kitten—!" she cried, shoving through a break in the hedge.

"I—I'm sorry," I stammered. "I didn't know. I—"

"Where did you find her?" the woman demanded, her face still bright red.

"In . . . in the hedge."

"Oh, thank you! Thank you!" the woman said. She took the kitten from my hands and raised it to her cheek. "Sasha, where did you go?"

I'm not in trouble, I finally realized. The woman is happy—not angry.

"Sasha has been missing for two days," the woman told me, pressing the kitten against her face. "I offered a reward and everything. I almost gave up hope."

I let out a long sigh of relief. "She was right there," I said, pointing. "In the hedge. I think she was caught in it."

"Well, she's fine now, thanks to you." Still pressing the kitten to her cheek, the woman pushed through the hedge and started to the house. "What is your name?"

"Luke."

"Well, follow me, Luke. I'll get your reward for you."

"Huh? Reward? No. Really," I started to back away.

"You saved Sasha's life," the woman said. "You did a wonderful thing. And I insist you take the reward I offered."

I saw that I had no choice. I followed her to her kitchen door.

A few minutes later she counted out five twenty-dollar bills and pressed them into my hand. "Thank you, Luke. You really did your good deed for today!"

A hundred dollars!

A hundred dollars reward!

My luck really is starting to change, I decided.

When I got home, a big surprise awaited me.

Mom had made my favorite dinner—meat loaf, mashed potatoes, and gravy. And a coconut cake for dessert!

"It's not even my birthday!" I exclaimed.

"I just felt like doing something nice for you today," Mom said. She brushed back my hair with one hand. "I know Friday the thirteenth is always a hard day for you."

"Not today!" I told her, grinning. "Not today!"

After my second slice of coconut cake, I went up to my room and started my homework. I spent about an hour writing out the answers to my science assignment.

It shouldn't have taken that long. But I kept taking out the twenty-dollar bills, counting them again, and dreaming about what I could buy with them.

After science I worked on my computer animation. I'd been having trouble with the last section. I couldn't get anything to move the way I wanted.

But tonight my good luck continued. I had no trouble at all. The images all slid together perfectly. I almost finished the project.

A little after nine I decided to give Hannah a call. She'd acted so weird at lunch that afternoon. I thought maybe she was sick or something.

I called to see if she was feeling better. But I could tell by the way she answered the phone that she still wasn't her old self.

I tried to cheer her up. I told her about my triumph at basketball practice. And about the hundred-dollar reward for finding the lost kitten.

"Very cool," Hannah said. But her voice showed no enthusiasm at all.

"And then Mom made all of my favorite things for dinner!" I exclaimed.

"Lucky," Hannah muttered.

"What's your problem?" I demanded. "What's wrong with you today?"

A long silence at her end.

Finally she said, "I guess I'm just in a bad mood. I fell off my bike on the way home this afternoon."

I groaned. "Oh, no. Are you okay?"

"Not really," she replied. "I scraped all the skin off my right hand. And I twisted my ankle pretty bad."

"Wow," I muttered. "Bad news."

"Especially since I have a basketball game tomorrow," Hannah sighed.

"Think you'll be able to play?" I asked.

"Maybe," she said glumly.

"Maybe I'll come watch your game," I said.

There was a long silence. And then Hannah said, "Luke, there's something . . . something I have to tell you."

"Excuse me?" I said. She was whispering, so low I could barely hear her.

"I really should tell you something. But . . ."

I pressed the phone tighter to my ear. "What? What is it?"

"Well . . ."

Another long silence.

"I can't," she said finally. I heard a click, and the line went silent.

The next morning my good luck came to an end.

At least, I *thought* my good luck had ended.

When I arrived at my science class, I searched my backpack for the homework questions. Not there. I took everything out—every paper, every book, every pencil.

Not there. I had spent over an hour on that assignment last night. And I'd left it at home.

Now I was in major trouble. Miss Creamer didn't accept late homework. And homework counted for fifty percent of the grade in her class.

My stomach tightened with dread as she entered the science lab to begin class.

How could I be so stupid?

"Good morning, everyone," she began. "I have an announcement to make. It's about last night's homework."

The room grew silent.

"I have to apologize to all of you," Miss Creamer continued. "I gave the wrong assignment. Those weren't the right questions. I'm really sorry. You don't have to turn it in. Just tear it up and throw it away."

Cheers rang out. Some kids gleefully ripped their papers into shreds. A big celebration.

Yes! More good luck for me, I thought happily.

I was on a hot streak. Later, when Miss Creamer handed back last week's test, I had the only A in the class.

In the lunchroom I grabbed the *last* slice of pizza on the counter!

All the kids behind me in line groaned. Darnell came up and offered to pay me five dollars for it. But no deal.

After school I stopped by the computer lab to see Mrs. Coffey. She told me her plans had suddenly changed. She wouldn't be leaving school for another two weeks.

I cheered. That meant I had time to finish my computer animation project and show it to her before I left.

"Luke, I was talking about you to my friend who owns Linkups. You know—the computer store on Highlands? I told him about how you can do anything with computers, fix them, upgrade them. He said you might be able to come into the store on Saturdays and help out in the service department."

I gasped. "Really?"

She nodded. "He's a really nice guy, and he's always looking for people who can fix machines. He said he couldn't give you a real job since you're only twelve. But he could pay you five dollars an hour."

"Wow! I cried. "That's awesome! Thanks, Mrs. Coffey."

I practically flew down the stairs to the gym. I wanted to flap my arms and take off! So many great things were happening to me! I couldn't believe it!

Hannah's basketball game had already started when I stepped into the gym. I found a seat in the bleachers and glanced up at the scoreboard. The Squirettes were already losing ten to two.

What's going on? I wondered. How can Hannah's team be losing so badly? The team they were playing—the Bee Stingers from Elwood Middle School—were the worst team in the city!

I turned and glanced around the bleachers. There were only about twenty kids watching the game. And four or five parents, clustered together at the top of the bleachers.

"Go, Sharon!" one of the mothers yelled.

But the gym was pretty quiet. I guess because the Squirettes were playing so badly.

I leaned forward and tried to concentrate on the game.

Sharon McCombs, the tallest girl in the Shawnee Valley eighth grade, tossed the ball in. A pass. Then another pass, which was almost stolen by a Bee Stinger.

Hannah grabbed the ball. She turned and started

to dribble to the basket. After about three steps she tripped. The ball bounced away as she fell flat on her stomach.

A Bee Stinger grabbed it just before it went out of bounds. She dribbled all the way down the floor—and scored easily before Hannah had even picked herself up off the floor. Twelve to two.

I cupped my hands around my mouth. "Get 'em, Hannah!" I shouted.

She didn't look up. She was fiddling with the white bandage on her hand.

A minute later Hannah had the ball again. In close. She jumped and shot. And missed. Missed the net, the backboard. Missed everything.

I leaned on my hands and watched the game in silence. Hannah missed six or seven shots in a row. She tripped over the ball, hit the floor hard, and got a huge, bright red floor burn on her knee. Her passes to her teammates went wild. She kept losing the ball to the other team. Tripping over her own feet. Bumping into other players.

It was sad. She didn't look like Hannah at all.

The half-time score was Bee Stingers twenty-five, Squirettes five.

When the team came out to start the second half, Hannah sat down on the bench and didn't play.

What's going on? I wondered.

I climbed down from the bleachers and walked over to her on the bench.

"Luke, you came to a bad-news game," she said, shaking her head.

"What's wrong?" I asked. "You're hurt? From your bike accident yesterday?"

She watched the Bee Stingers score another basket. Then she turned to me. "No. It's not because of my accident," she whispered. Her eyes were dull, watery. Her skin was so pale.

"So, what is it?" I asked.

Hannah frowned. "It's all because I lost my good-luck charm," she said.

I gaped at her. "Huh?"

"It's what brought me all that amazing great luck," Hannah said. "I have to find it. As soon as I lost it, my luck changed."

My mouth dropped open. I realized my heart had started to pound.

"It's a tiny skull," Hannah continued. "A little yellow skull. I—I never went anywhere without it."

She tugged at the bandage on her hand. Then she raised her eyes to me. "You haven't seen it anywhere . . . have you, Luke?"

My legs suddenly felt weak. I gripped the back of the bench and stared at Hannah. I could feel my face growing red.

I could feel the skull in my jeans pocket. I knew I should pull it out and hand it to her.

But how *could* I?

I needed the good luck, too. Hannah had enjoyed so much good luck for so long. Mine had just started. For the first time in my life, I was having a little good luck.

How could I go back to being a loser again?

Hannah's watery eyes locked on mine. "Have you seen it, Luke?" she repeated. "Have you seen it anywhere?"

My face burned. So many frantic thoughts whirred through my head.

I really needed that good-luck charm. Ever since I found it, my life had changed. I was a new person.

But Hannah was my friend. My best friend in the

whole world. She was always there for me when I needed her.

I couldn't lie to her—could I?

"No," I said. "I haven't seen it anywhere."

Hannah's eyes remained on me for a few seconds more. Then she nodded slowly and turned back to the game.

My heart was pounding hard now. I had a heavy feeling in the pit of my stomach. "Where did you lose it?" I asked.

She didn't reply. She cupped her hands around her mouth and cheered on her teammates.

I backed away from the bench. I felt like a total creep. I jammed my hand into my pocket. Wrapped my fingers around the rubber skull.

Give it back to her, Luke, a voice in my head urged. The voice of goodness. The voice of friendship.

But I knew I wasn't going to give it back. I was already trotting out of the gym and down the hall to the exit.

I need it a little while longer, I told myself. Just a little while.

Long enough to win the basketball championship. Long enough to get really good grades for the first time in my life. Long enough to impress my friends . . . to get on the swim team . . . to make a name for myself . . . long enough to be a *winner.*

I squeezed the little skull all the way home. I'll

give it back to Hannah in a couple of weeks, I told myself. Two weeks, that's all. Maybe three. And then I'll give it back to her. And she can have her good luck again. No harm done.

No harm done—right?

The phone was ringing when I stepped in the kitchen door. I tossed down my backpack and ran to answer it.

To my surprise, it was Mrs. Coffey.

"Luke, I'm glad I caught you," she said. "I have some really good news. You know my friend at the computer store?"

"Yes?"

"I spoke to him after you left the computer lab. And he said you could start work at his store on Saturday."

"That's great!" I exclaimed.

"But that's not my good news," Mrs. Coffey continued. "He has a friend who is putting together a show of computer animation. And his friend is very interested in seeing your work."

"Really?" I cried.

"He needs short pieces for his animation show right away," she said. "If he likes your piece, he said he will pay a thousand dollars for it."

"Wow!"

"Is it finished, Luke?" Mrs. Coffey asked. "Is it ready to show to him?"

I thought hard. "Almost," I said. "I need two more days on it. Maybe three."

"Well, try to hurry," Mrs. Coffey said. "I think he has most of the pieces he needs. He's going to be showing them all over the country. It would be a shame to miss out—"

"It sure would!" I interrupted. "I'll get right to work on it, Mrs. Coffey. And thanks. Thanks a lot!"

Excited, I hurried up to my room and turned on the computer. Maybe I can get some work done on it before dinner, I decided.

I heard Mom come in downstairs. I called hi to her and said I was working on my computer project.

A few minutes later the phone rang again. I heard Mom talking for a while. Then I heard her running up the stairs. She burst into my room, ran up behind me, and wrapped me in a big hug.

"Huh? What's that for?" I cried.

"That was Mario's Steakhouse on the phone," Mom said, grinning. "You know. Your favorite restaurant. You won, Luke! Remember that drawing we all entered the last time we were there? Well, you won it. They picked your card. You won dinner for the whole family. Twelve dinners! One a month for the next year!"

"Wow!" I jumped up from the computer. Laughing and cheering, Mom and I did a happy little dance around the room.

"I can't believe you won that drawing. That is so

terrific!" Mom exclaimed. "We're going to have to start calling you Lucky Luke!"

"Yeah. Lucky Luke," I repeated. "I like that. That's me. Lucky Luke."

I worked on my animation until nearly midnight. I stared into the glow of the monitor until I couldn't see straight, and the images became a fuzzy blur.

"Almost finished," I said, yawning.

I changed into pajamas, brushed my teeth, got ready for sleep. But just before I climbed into bed, I pulled out my lucky little skull for one last look.

I held it gently in my hand and studied it, rubbing my fingers over the smooth top of the skull. The tiny, red jewel eyes glowed brightly.

I rubbed my fingers over the hard, bumpy teeth. I twirled the skull in my hand.

"My little good-luck charm," I whispered.

I set it down carefully on my dresser, in front of the mirror. Then I turned out the lights and climbed into bed.

I settled back on my pillows, pulling the quilt up to my chin. I yawned loudly. The mattress creaked under me. Waiting for sleep, I stared into the darkness.

The curtains were pulled, so no light washed in from the street. The room was completely black, except for a faint red glow.

The glow of the two red eyes in the skull. Like tiny

match flames against the blackness.

And then I saw two more glowing spots of red light. Larger. Behind the tiny skull eyes.

Two circles of light in the mirror glass. Two flame-red circles, the size of tennis balls.

And as their light grew brighter, more intense . . . I could see a form in the dresser mirror.

Deep nostril holes . . . two rows of jagged, grinning teeth.

A skull. A red-eyed skull.

Not tiny. A huge, grinning, yellow-boned skull that *filled* the mirror!

Filled the mirror! And stared out at me with those fiery, flame-red eyes.

I sat straight up. Squeezed the quilt. And gaped in horror as the jagged teeth moved. The jaw slid open.

And the enormous skull mouthed the words . . . mouthed them so clearly . . .

"Lucky Luke."

The giant, glowing skull leaned forward, as if to push out of the mirror. The jaw worked up and down. The red glow seemed to bathe the whole room in flames.

I opened my mouth in a horrified scream.

I screamed and then screamed again.

The ceiling light flashed on.

"Luke—what's wrong?"

Blinking in the sudden light, I saw my dad burst breathlessly into the room. His pajama shirt was twisted. One pajama pants leg rode up to his knee. His hair was tangled from sleep, standing straight up on one side.

"What is it?" he repeated.

"I—I—" I pointed to the mirror. My head spun with confusion. I couldn't find words.

"The skull—" I finally choked out.

Brushing back his hair, Dad crossed the room to my dresser.

I stared into the glass.

Nothing now.

Nothing in there, except the reflection of my room. As he came near, I could see Dad's worried face reflected in the glass.

"Is *this* what you were screaming about?" Dad asked. He picked up the little yellow skull and held it out to me. "This skull?"

"N-no," I stammered.

I was thinking hard, trying to figure out what I had seen.

It couldn't have been the reflection of the little skull I saw in the glass.

No.

The skull that loomed in the mirror was enormous, its eyes as big as basketballs!

Dad still squinted at me from the dresser, holding the little skull up in front of him.

"I guess I had a bad dream," I said softly, settling back onto my pillows. "It—it was so weird. I dreamed I saw a giant skull with flaming eyes. But . . . it was so real!"

Dad shook his head. "Well . . . if this little skull is giving you bad dreams, want me to take it away?" He started to the door.

"No!" I screamed.

I jumped out of bed to block his path. He looked startled as I grabbed the skull from his hand.

"It's . . . it's a good-luck charm," I said. "It's brought me a lot of good luck."

Dad frowned as he gazed at the little skull in my hand. "You sure, Luke? It doesn't look good to me. It looks evil."

"Evil?" I laughed. "No way, Dad. No way. Trust me."

He clicked off the light on his way out. A short while later, I fell asleep gripping the skull tightly in one hand.

A few days later I screamed my head off again.

This time it was for fun.

A bunch of us were on our skates up on Killer Hill. It's actually Miller Hill. But we call it Killer Hill because it's up at the top where Broad Street scoops straight down—a steep, steep slope down three blocks to Miller Street.

Miller Street has the most traffic in Shawnee Valley. So the idea is, we come skating down Broad Street full speed. We come rocketing down the steep slope as fast as we can—and try to skate right through the traffic on Miller.

It makes all the car drivers totally crazy! You can always hear tires squealing, horns honking, drivers screaming as kids come skating right at them.

Yes. It's really dangerous. Most kids won't even *think* of trying it. But for a guy with my kind of good luck, what's the big deal?

It was a sunny, cold Sunday afternoon. Frost stuck to the tops of the cars. My breath smoked up in front of me as I skated to the top of Killer Hill.

I met Darnell up there. He was having trouble with the brake on one of his skates. Finally he just ripped the brake off and tossed it in a trash can. "Why do I need brakes?" he said, grinning at me. "They only slow you down."

Stretch and some of his pals appeared a few minutes later. Stretch was wearing some kind of yellow sweats. He looked like Big Bird on skates!

He lowered his shoulder and tried to bump me off my feet. But I skated away easily. And he didn't try again.

Things have been a little different between Stretch and me since I took his place on the basketball team. He's *my* backup now. He gets to play only when I'm tired and need a short rest. And I think he's in shock over it.

Stretch still tries to give me a hard time. But I don't think his heart is in it. He knows he's a loser. He knows he's not one of the lucky people—like me.

"You ready to skate?" Darnell called. He pulled on his helmet. Then he stood in the middle of the street, leaning forward, hands on his knees.

I gazed down the steep hill to the traffic below. Even though it was Sunday afternoon, cars and vans sped along Miller as if it were the afternoon rush hour.

I adjusted my knee pads. "Ready," I said. I moved beside Darnell.

Stretch skated in front of us. He grinned at me.

"How about a race?"

I shook my head. "You're too slow. Darnell and I don't want to have to wait for you down there."

"Ha ha. When did you get so funny, Champ?" Stretch reached into the pocket of his yellow sweats. He held up a ten-dollar bill. "Let's make it a real race. Ten bucks each. Winner takes all."

He stuck the money in front of my face. I shoved it away. "I don't take candy from babies," I said. "Keep your money."

Stretch gritted his teeth. His pale face turned an angry red. He leaned close. "You gonna race me or not?" he growled.

I squeezed the rubber skull in my pocket. I knew there was no way I could lose. "Okay," I said. "But I'm going to make it fair."

I pulled a wool scarf from my coat pocket and started to wrap it around my head. "Just to give you a chance, I'll skate blindfolded."

Stretch snickered. "You're joking, right? You're going to skate through all those cars blindfolded?"

"Don't do it, Luke!" a voice called.

I turned to see Hannah waving to me. She was hobbling up the sidewalk on crutches. Her right foot had a large, white bandage over it. "Don't do it!" she called shrilly.

I spun away from the guys and skated over to her.

"Hannah—what happened?" I asked, motioning to the crutches.

She sighed and leaned heavily on them. "It's my ankle," she said. "Remember when I fell off my bike? We thought it was just a sprain. But my ankle keeps swelling up like a water balloon. I had to have it drained three times."

"Yuck," I said, staring down at the bandage.

The wind fluttered her red hair. She shook her head sadly. "The doctors can't figure out what's wrong. I—I might need surgery. I don't know. And Mom says if it doesn't get better, I can't go on the junior high overnight on Wednesday."

"Wow. That's bad news," I murmured. Everyone looks forward to the overnight. The whole junior high goes to a campground by the lake, and everyone stays up and parties all night.

I couldn't take my eyes off Hannah's bandaged ankle. Is this my fault? I suddenly wondered. Did I really take away her good luck? Hannah has had nothing but bad luck ever since I found the skull. . . .

I'm going to give it back to her, I silently promised. Real soon. Real soon.

"You skating or not?" Stretch called. "Or are you just going to stand there and talk with your girl-friend?"

"I'm coming," I said. I started to wrap the scarf around my eyes.

"Luke, don't," Hannah insisted. "Don't do it blindfolded. It—it's crazy."

"No problem," I said. "I'm a superhero, Hannah. Cars will bounce right off me!"

I skated away from her.

"You're wrong!" she called. "Luke, listen to me. The good luck—it doesn't last forever!"

I laughed. What was she *talking* about?

I skated up beside Darnell and grabbed his arm to steady myself. I pulled the scarf over my eyes until I saw only black.

"You're crazy," he muttered. "You could get killed, man."

"No way," I declared. "I'm going to win twenty bucks from you two!"

I heard Stretch skate up beside me. "You're doing this for real?" he asked. "You're going to skate into all those cars blindfolded?"

"You going to talk or skate?" I asked him. "First one past Miller Street *without stopping* wins the money."

"Luke—don't be crazy!" Hannah called.

It was the last thing I heard before the three of us took off.

I leaned forward, skating straight and hard. I heard Stretch and Darnell beside me, their Rollerblades scraping the pavement.

As we picked up speed, I could hear the traffic on Miller. I heard a horn honk. Heard someone shout.

I skated down . . . down . . . laughing through the darkness.

"Luke—loooook out!"

I heard Darnell's scream. I heard the squeal of tires. Horns honked.

I tossed back my head and laughed. I roared through Miller Street, the blade wheels whistling over the pavement.

Then, as I turned my skates and came to a slow stop, I ripped the scarf away. And saw Darnell standing on the curb on the other side of Miller. His mouth was open. He shook his head.

Stretch came skating around me. "You crazy jerk!" he shouted. "You were almost killed *three* times!"

I calmly held out my hand. "Money, please."

"You lucky jerk," Stretch muttered. He slapped the ten-dollar bill into my gloved hand. "You're crazy. Really. You're just plain crazy."

I laughed. "Thanks for the compliment! And the ten bucks!"

Grumbling to himself, Stretch skated back up to his friends.

Darnell waited for the traffic to clear, then skated over to me. He wiped sweat off his forehead. "You were almost killed," he said, his voice shaking. "Why did you do it, Luke?"

I grinned at him. "Because I can."

The weather turned warm for our overnight campout. Even though the trees were bare, the woods smelled fresh and sweet, almost like spring. High, white clouds dotted the bright blue afternoon sky. Twigs and dead leaves crackled and crunched under our feet as we hiked through the tall trees to the camping grounds.

I squeezed the small skull in one hand as I walked, weighted down by the heavy pack on my back. Some kids were singing a Beatles song. Behind me, a group of girls were telling really bad knock-knock jokes, laughing shrilly after each one.

Coach Bendix and Ms. Raymond, another gym teacher, led the way along the twisting path through the trees. I was about halfway back in the line of kids.

I turned and found Hannah beside me. She wore her blue windbreaker with the hood pulled up over her head. She was leaning on one crutch as she walked, struggling to keep up. "Do you have any water?" she asked.

I slowed down. "Your parents let you come? Is your ankle better?"

"Not really," she replied, frowning. "But I told them I had to come anyway. I wouldn't miss it. Do you have any water? I'm dying!"

"Yeah. Sure." I reached for the bottle of water in my pack. "Didn't you bring any?"

Hannah sighed. "My water bottle had a leak or something. It poured out and soaked all the extra clothes in my pack. Now I don't have a thing to wear."

I handed her the water bottle.

Leaning on the crutch, she pushed back the windbreaker hood, and I saw her face for the first time.

Her skin was covered with big, red splotches.

"Hannah, what's that?" I cried. "Your face—"

"Don't look at me!" she snapped. She turned her back and took a long gulp of water.

"But what is it?" I demanded. "Poison ivy?"

"No. I don't think so," she said, still facing away from me. "I woke up with it. Some kind of red rash. All over my body." She sighed. "I don't get a break."

She handed the water bottle back to me and pulled the blue plastic hood over her head. "Thanks for the water."

"Does it itch?" I asked.

She let out an angry cry. "I really don't want to talk about it!" She grabbed the crutch tightly, swung it hard in front of her, and hurried ahead of me, dragging her bandaged foot over the dirt path.

She's having so much bad luck. I guess it's my fault, I thought, squeezing the skull in my pocket.

But *why* are all these terrible things happening to her? Why isn't there enough good luck for *both* of us?

I didn't have much time to think about it.

Behind me, I heard shrill, frightened screams. I saw kids running off the path. Screaming. Calling for help.

I spun around and headed toward them, the heavy pack bouncing on my back. "What's going on?" I cried. "What's wrong?"

More shrill screams.

And then I saw the two enormous brown snakes. Swinging down from a low tree limb. Blocking the path.

The same color as the tree, they twisted their long bodies, thicker than garden hoses, and snapped their jaws.

I didn't hesitate. I dived forward, stretching out my arms.

"Luke—what are you doing? Stay away from them!" I heard Coach Bendix shout.

The kids' frightened screams rang through the woods.

"Get away from them!" Coach ordered.

But I knew nothing could hurt me. I knew my good luck would keep me safe.

I shot my hands out. And grabbed both snakes, one in each hand.

I wrapped my fingers around their thick bodies. Then, with a hard tug, I wrenched them off the tree limb. And raised them high.

"Whoa!"

I didn't realize how *long* they were.

And how strong.

I let out a startled cry as both snakes wriggled loose. I saw the tiny, black eyes flash. Saw the jaws open.

Then both snake heads came crashing toward me, jaws snapping—snapping so furiously beneath the flashing eyes, snapping like bear traps.

I felt a rush of air as they snapped—snapped—snapped their sharp-toothed jaws. Heads swinging wildly. Whole bodies swinging and shaking. Thick, white drool clinging to their pointed teeth.

Shrill screams rose all around me. I stared at the snapping heads, the glimmering, black eyes—until it seemed that the snakes were screaming, too.

And then—they flew from my hands.

Wriggled free with strong tosses of their heavy bodies. And plunged to the ground. Disappearing so quickly. Blending into the hard, brown dirt. Vanishing beneath the carpet of fat brown leaves, twigs, and fallen limbs.

As kids surrounded me, I stood hunched over, gasping for breath. I smoothed my open hands over my ears, my cheeks, my whole face.

I waited for the pain of the snakebites to spread over me.

But no. No sting. No throbbing. No pain.

They had snapped so close, I felt their breath on my skin.

But they hadn't bitten me.

"You're so lucky!" Coach Bendix was saying. He had a hand on my shoulder and was examining my face. "I never saw anyone so lucky. Why did you do it, Luke? Those snakes are deadly poisonous. Deadly! Why did you do it?"

I stared at him but didn't answer. I didn't know what to say.

How could I explain it to him? How could I explain to *anyone* what it felt like to be so incredibly, awesomely lucky?

All around, kids were cheering. Congratulating me. Talking about me, how brave I had been.

Leaning against a tree, I saw Hannah. She stood by herself, crutch under one arm. She was the only one not smiling, not cheering.

I saw the red blotches on Hannah's face. Watched as she transfered the crutch to her other arm. And saw her scowling at me, her eyes narrowed. She shook her head and scowled.

And in that moment, I realized that she was *jealous*. Jealous of my good luck.

Jealous that she was no longer the hero. *She* was no longer the lucky one.

Too bad, Hannah, I thought, watching her angry expression. I had felt sorry for her. I had felt really *guilty*, too.

But no more.

I've got the luck now, Hannah, I thought. *And I'm going to keep it*!

"Let's go, guys. We've got another game to win!" I cried. I gave Sam Mulroney a playful towel slap.

Locker doors slammed. Guys finished lacing up their basketball shoes.

"Did you *see* those Deaver Mills guys?" Mulroney asked, peeking into the gym through a crack in the locker room door. "They're *monsters*! They must feed those guys whole steaks five times a day!"

"Big doesn't mean good!" I said. "They look like cows! They're so slow."

"We'll dribble circles around them!" Jay Boxer said.

"Just feed me the ball!" I instructed them. "No matter where I am. Feed me the ball. I'll put it in. I'm feeling lucky today, guys. Real lucky!"

"Hey, Champ—" Stretch called, pulling on his jersey. "You're not a ball hog or anything—are you?"

Guys used to laugh when Stretch shouted insults at me. But not anymore. Everyone was on my side now. Everyone wanted to be on the *winner's* side.

"Hey, Stretch—what do they call *you*?" I shouted back. "A *bench* hog?"

Everybody laughed.

Stretch laughed too. Now that I was a winner, he was starting to be a little nicer to me. He even gave me some dribbling tips after one practice.

The guys all headed out to the gym. I could hear the shouts of the crowd in the bleachers. And the steady *thud* of basketballs on the floor as the Deaver Mills Lions warmed up.

"Time to kill me some Lions," I muttered. I finished lacing my sneakers.

Then I stood up. Started to swing my gym locker closed.

And slammed my left hand in the door.

"Hey!" I cried out in surprise as pain shot up my arm.

I shook the hand hard, trying to shake the pain away. My wrist throbbed. I moved my fingers, tilted my hand back and forth. It moved okay. Not broken.

But the hand was red and already starting to swell.

"No time for this," I muttered.

I slammed the locker shut with my right hand. And, still shaking my left hand, hurried out into the gym.

The crowd cheered as I ran onto the floor. I saw some of the Deaver Mills players whisper to each other and point at me. They knew who the star player was. They knew who was going to *wipe the floor* with them today!

We huddled close around Coach Bendix. "Take it slow with these guys," he instructed. "Feel them out. Get their rhythm. Let's rattle them, show them we can play defense."

"Just get me the ball!" I chimed in. "I'm going to be loose under the basket all day!"

We gave our team cheer and trotted out to the center of the floor. I searched the bleachers for Hannah. She said she would try to come to the game today.

I spotted her at the side of the bleachers, hunched in a wheelchair. Her bad foot was propped up, and it had an even bigger bandage over it.

I guess it isn't getting better, I thought. I felt a pang of guilt.

Poor Hannah.

I looked for my parents. Then I remembered they weren't coming today. They had to stay home for a furniture delivery.

I turned away from the crowd. I had a game to play. Time to get my game face on. No time to think about Hannah and her problems.

I went up for the opening jump. I tapped the ball to Mulroney, and the game was underway.

He dribbled to half-court, then sent a high pass to me.

"Whoa—!" The ball flew right through my hands and bounced out of bounds.

"Mulroney—too hard!" I called. "Who were you throwing at?"

He shrugged and started trotting to the Lions' basket.

"Get in there, Luke! Get going! Look alive!" I heard Coach Bendix shouting.

The Deaver guard came dribbling slowly toward me. I darted up to him, stuck out my hand to steal the ball—and missed.

He moved past me easily and sent up an easy layup for two points.

"Weird," I muttered. I shook my left hand. The pain had dulled to an ache, but the hand was pretty swollen.

I moved down the court. Caught a pass. Spun away from the Lion defender. Went in for an easy shot.

And missed!

"Huh?"

I heard the crowd groan. Startled voices all around.

Mulroney slapped me on the shoulder. "Take it easy, man," he said. "Play your game. Just play your game."

A few seconds later I drove in for a shot—and was fouled. I moved to the foul line—and missed both foul shots!

More groans and muttering from the bleachers. I saw Coach Bendix shake his head.

A bounce pass from Jay Boxer sailed right through my legs. Some of the Lions' players had a good laugh over that one.

Then I missed three more shots in a row!

Mulroney flashed me a thumbs-up. "No prob," he called. "Play your game, Luke! We'll get 'em!"

The Lions were winning twelve to four.

I took another pass and moved under the basket. I

leaped high for a slam dunk.

My arm hit the rim hard. I cried out in pain. And watched the ball sail over the backboard.

"Whoa. This isn't happening," I muttered, picking myself up off the floor. "No way."

At the other end of the floor I grabbed a rebound off the backboard. I dodged past a huge Lion player. Dribbled away from him easily. Picked up speed. Brought the ball onto our side of the court.

Eyed the basket. Prepared to stop short and put up a three-pointer.

And tripped. Felt one sneaker bump the other. Tripped over my own shoe.

And watched the ball sail into a Lion's hands as I stumbled. I fell forward onto my stomach. My arms and legs were out flat on the floor. "OOOF!"

I heard startled gasps from the bleachers. And laughter.

Yes. Some people were laughing at me.

"What is going on?" I cried.

I forced myself to my feet. Shook off the pain.

"This isn't happening. It can't be!"

I reached into the pocket of my uniform shorts. Reached for my good-luck skull.

Fumbled in the pocket. Searched both pockets.

"Hey—"

No. No. No way.

The skull was gone!

Fumbling frantically in both pockets, I began running for the team bench. "Time out! Time out!" I screamed.

Had the skull fallen out of my pocket?

I squinted hard, searching the gleaming, polished floor.

No sign of it.

"Time out!" I pleaded.

I heard a whistle blow on the sidelines.

I had to find it—now! I couldn't play without it.

My eyes swept over the floor. I began to run full speed to the bench.

I didn't see the huge Lions player—until we collided.

I plowed right into him. Caught him flat-footed. He let out a startled, "Oof." And we cracked heads.

"Yaaaiiii!" I let out a scream of agony as blinding red pain shot around my head. The red shimmered to gold. Brighter, brighter . . . bright as the sun.

I felt my legs giving out. Felt myself collapsing, crumbling into a deep, deep, bottomless darkness.

I woke up to pinpoints of yellow light. They flickered high above me. Each time they flashed, a wave of pain rolled over my forehead, down the back of my neck.

I blinked hard. Blinked until I realized I was staring up at the lights on the gym rafters.

I lay on my back on the gym floor, one knee raised, my hands flat at my sides. I squinted up at the high rafters—until faces blocked my view.

Players' faces. And then a few worried-looking adults. And then Coach Bendix's face, looming over me, bobbing over me like a parade balloon.

"What—?" One word escaped my throat. My dry throat. So dry, I couldn't swallow.

"Stay still, Luke," Coach ordered, speaking softly. His dark eyes peered down into mine, studying me. "You've had a bad concussion. Don't try to move. We're sending you to the emergency room."

"Huh? No!" I gasped.

I rolled onto my side. I lurched to my feet. The floor tilted from side to side, as if I were on a rocking boat.

"Don't move, Luke." Coach reached for me.

But I staggered out of his grasp. Stumbled through the circle of people that had formed around me.

"No. No hospital!" I croaked.

I had to find that skull. That was all I needed, and then I would be okay again.

The skull . . .

I stumbled over someone's shoe. Staggered toward the locker room. The gleaming wood floor swaying beneath me.

"Luke—come back!"

No. No way. I shoved open the locker room door with one shoulder. And sliding a hand against the lockers, moved to the back row. Lurched to my gym locker. Pulled open the door so hard it slammed against the frame.

"Where is it? Where?"

I frantically pawed through my street clothes. Searched and then tossed everything onto the floor.

"Where? Where?"

Not in my khakis pockets. Not in my shirt pocket. Not in my sweatshirt.

The locker floor? No. Nothing down there.

Stumbling over the pile of clothes on the floor, I lurched back down the row of gym lockers. Ran through the gym, out the doors, and up the stairs. Into the long, empty hall.

My sneakers squeaked on the hard floor as I ran. The walls and ceiling appeared to close in on me, then slide back into place.

To my locker. To locker 13.

It took me three tries to get the combination right. But finally I unlocked it and flung open the door.

And jammed my hand into one coat pocket, and then the other.

"Where is it? I have to have it! Where? Where?"

And then a long, happy sigh escaped my parched throat as my hand closed around it.

Yessss!

I was so happy!

I had the skull in my hand. I squeezed it tightly. So happy. So happy.

I pulled it out of the coat pocket. Raised it in front of me. Raised it close to examine it.

And let out a cry of horror.

The eyes. They were dark. Not red, not glowing.

And the face had *changed*! The bump-toothed grin was gone. The open mouth was curled down in a fierce, angry scowl.

"No—it's impossible!" I gasped.

I held the skull up to the light. The red jewel eyes were gone! The deep, round sockets were empty. The skull scowled down at me, dark and menacing.

What does this mean? I wondered. How did this happen?

Before I could think about it clearly, I glimpsed something in the open locker. A soft glow. A slow moving light, growing larger as if moving closer.

The light split into two. Two circles of red light. Down low. Very low, near the locker floor.

I gripped the skull tightly in my fist and stared as the red lights glimmered closer. The whole locker shimmered. The dark walls reflected the two lights. Brighter . . . bright as fire now.

Two red eyes, I realized. Two glowing eyes floating from the blackness of locker 13.

I jumped back as a black cat stepped silently out, as if floating. A black cat with fiery, red eyes. The same black cat as before?

It pulled back its lips, bared pointed, white teeth, and hissed at me.

My back hit the wall. I blinked against the brightness of those two circles of red light.

And as I trembled in horror, squeezing the skull, squeezing it so tightly my hand ached—the cat rose up off the floor.

And melted into another form.

Melted and grew taller. Taller . . . The cat became a human figure, dressed all in black, wrapped in a broad, black coat down to the floor, its face hidden in the darkness of a black hood.

Hidden. All hidden . . . except for the eyes—those horrifying, fiery eyes.

"Wh-who are you? What do you want?" I startled myself by crying out those words. I didn't think I could speak.

My whole body trembled. I pressed myself against the wall to keep from falling to my knees.

The hooded figure stepped silently away from the open locker. A hoarse rasp burst out from under the hood, a whisper like the crackle of dead leaves: "*The luck has run out, Luke.*"

"No!" I gasped.

A bony hand swung out from the sleeve of the black coat—and swiped the skull away from me.

"No!" I cried in protest. "No! No!"

"The luck is over."

"Who are you?" I shrieked in a tight, terrified voice. "Wh-who? How did you get in my locker? What do you want?" I screamed in total panic.

"The luck is over."

"It can't be!" I cried. "It can't be! I need it!"

"*Over . . .*" the hooded figure rasped. "*Over . . . over . . .*"

The red eyes glowed from under the hood. The bony hand held the tiny skull in front of the broad black coat.

"I need that luck!" I wailed. "I need that skull!"

And I grabbed it back. Grabbed it out of the bony hand.

"I need it! I *have* to have it!"

I raised the skull in front of me. Stared hard at it.

What was *wrong* with it? Something wriggling on it . . . wriggling in my hand . . . crawling over my palm . . .

"Ohhhh." I let out a moan as I saw. The skull was covered . . . crawling . . . crawling with hundreds of maggots!

The skull fell from my hand and bounced across the floor. I frantically shook my hand, scraped it against the wall, brushing the disgusting maggots off my skin.

Under the black hood the red eyes glowed brighter. *"You enjoyed a lot of good luck, Luke,"* the figure said in his hoarse croak. *"But the luck has ended. And now you must pay for it."*

"Huh? Pay?" I felt my throat tighten. I stared at the fiery eyes, trying to see a face, trying to see who was speaking to me from under that hood.

"Luke—I'm so sorry!" a voice called.

I turned to find Hannah wheeling herself rapidly down the hall, leaning forward in her wheelchair, turning the wheels with both hands.

"Hannah—? What—?" I couldn't find any words.

"I'm so sorry," she repeated. As she wheeled herself closer, I saw tears brimming in her eyes, rolling down her red-blotched face.

"Sorry?" I repeated, my head spinning in confusion.

"He made me do it!" she wailed. "You have to believe me, Luke. I didn't want to. Really! But he made me!"

She grabbed my hand. Squeezed it tightly. Her hand was as cold as ice. Tears rolled down her cheeks.

"*Very touching!*" the hooded figure rasped coldly.

"Hannah—he made you do *what*?" I asked.

"He—he made me give you the skull!" Hannah stammered, still squeezing my hand.

"Huh?" I let out a startled cry. "You *gave* it to me? But I thought I found it. I thought—"

"I had the good luck for a long time," Hannah said, wiping her wet cheeks with both hands. "Remember when I had so much good luck? Then it ran out. The skull went dark. And he forced me—he forced me to pass the skull on to you!"

I stared at her in disbelief. "But who is he?" I cried. "How can he do this?"

"*Haven't you guessed?*" the hooded figure boomed. The red eyes glowed like two angry suns. "*Haven't you figured it out yet, Luke? I am the Fate Master. I decide who has good luck and who has bad!*"

"No," I whispered. "That's . . . crazy."

"It's the truth," Hannah said, her voice breaking. "He controls me. And now you."

"*Luke,*" the evil figure whispered, lowering himself toward me. "*Did you really think you could have all that good luck without paying for it?*"

"I didn't want to give the skull to you," Hannah whispered, holding on to my arm. "I gave you a chance to hand it back to me, remember? Remember during my game? I asked if you had seen it?"

I nodded sadly, feeling my face grow hot.

"I knew you had it. Why didn't you give it back then?" Hannah demanded. "I gave you a chance to return it. I didn't want you to keep it."

"Too late for that now!" the Fate Master rasped. *"Now you are BOTH mine!"*

"No way!" I protested. "I don't believe any of this! This can't be happening! It—it's some kind of bad joke!"

"It's not a joke," Hannah whispered. "Look at me." She pointed to her red-blotched face, her bandaged foot, the wheelchair.

"No!" I insisted. "It won't happen to me! I won't let it! I'll—I'll make my own luck!"

The bulky, black coat shook as the Fate Master uttered a hoarse laugh. It sounded more like dry coughing than laughter. *"Young man, do you really think you can go up against FATE? I control EVERYTHING that happens! Do you really think you can defy FATE?"*

"I don't care what you say!" I screamed. "I'm not going to be some kind of slave! You can't control me! You can't!"

The Fate Master sighed. The red eyes faded inside the hood. *"Do I really have to prove myself to you? Okay. So be it."*

He leaned closer. So close that I could see into the hood. I could see that he had no face! Just two glowing eyes floating in blackness.

"Luke—that concussion you had in the gym?" he rasped. *"I'm afraid it's much worse than you thought. Feel your ears."*

"Huh?" My hands shot up to my ears. I felt wetness.

Warm wetness.

I lowered my hands. My fingers dripped with blood.

My ears were bleeding!

I felt the warm blood pour down my earlobes, trickle down the sides of my face.

Frantically I pressed the palms of my hands against my ears.

"That won't stop the bleeding, Luke," the Fate Master whispered. *"That blood won't clot. It's just going to keep pouring out. Bad luck, I'm afraid. Very bad luck."*

"No—please!" I pleaded. "Make it stop!"

The eyes flared. *"Do you believe in me now? Do you believe that you belong to me?"*

"Okay," I said. "Okay. I believe you."

"Your fate is in my hands—both of you. You must pay for the good luck you had. You must suffer bad luck now—"

"No—please!" I begged. "I need more time. Things are just starting to go right for me. The basketball team . . . my animation . . . the swim team . . . I'll do anything. I need more time!"

"NO MORE TIME!" The hoarse rasp echoed off the tile walls. Angry flames shot out from the blackness of the hood.

"But—" I started, shrinking back beside Hannah.

"I control you!" the Fate Master boomed. *"I decide your luck from now on! Do you want me to go easy on the two of you? DO you?"*

"Y-yes," I stammered. "I'll do anything. Anything!"

The Fate Master was silent for a long moment. The eyes faded, as if retreating into the distance, then glowed brightly again. *"If you want me to go easy on you both," he said finally, "here's what you have to do. . . ."*

"Pass the skull on to another," the Fate Master ordered.

"Huh? You—you want me to give it to someone else?" I stammered.

The eyes sparked beneath the hood. *"Pass it to that big kid, the one called Stretch. I've had my eye on him. I will give him good luck for two months. Then I will claim him as mine."*

"No, I can't do that!" I protested. "It isn't right! It isn't—"

The Fate Master uttered a furious growl. *"Then you will suffer bad luck your whole life. You and everyone in your family!"*

I shivered in fear. My mind spun. I felt the warm blood start to trickle from my ears again.

Could I do it? Could I trap Stretch the way I had been trapped?

I felt Hannah tug my arm. "You have to do it, Luke," she whispered. "It's our only chance. Besides, Stretch has been asking for it—hasn't he? He's not a friend of yours. He's an enemy. Stretch has been asking for it all year."

True. Stretch wasn't my friend. But could I be responsible for ruining Stretch's life? For turning him over to the Fate Master?

Hannah gazed up at me from the wheelchair with pleading eyes. "Do it," she whispered. "Save us, Luke. Do it."

I turned to the Fate Master. "Okay," I choked out. "I'll do it."

The eyes flashed, from red to sunlight yellow. The big coat opened and appeared to fly up. It raised itself over me like giant bat wings. Floated over me . . . then floated down.

I felt myself covered in a heavy darkness.

I couldn't move. It spread over me . . . blacker . . . blacker.

I felt so cold. So cold and lost. As if I had been buried, buried deep in the cold, cold ground.

And then I blinked and saw pinpoints of light. Flickering white lights that grew brighter, so bright I had to squint.

It took me a while to realize I was back in the gym. Back on the gym floor. A crowd huddled around me. Tight expressions, worried faces.

Someone leaned over me. A face came into focus. Coach Bendix stared down at me, the whistle hanging from his neck.

"Coach—?" I tried to speak, but the word came out a whisper.

"Don't move, Luke," he said softly. "You've had a concussion, but you're going to be okay."

"A concussion?"

"Lie still," he instructed. "An ambulance is on the way."

A concussion?

It didn't happen! I realized.

The hooded figure with the glowing eyes. The Fate Master stepping out of locker 13. Taking away my good luck. Ordering me to pass the skull to Stretch.

It didn't happen!

It was a dream. A nightmare caused by my concussion.

I jumped to my feet. The floor swayed beneath me. The bleachers appeared to tilt to one side, then the other.

I saw Hannah in her wheelchair at the side of the bleachers.

She's still in the gym! I told myself happily. We never left the gym. It didn't happen. None of it happened.

I felt so happy. *So free*!

Before I even realized it, I was running. Running to the door.

"Luke! Hey—Luke! Stop!" I heard Coach Bendix calling to me.

And then I was out the gym doors. And racing through the dark, empty hallways. Running full speed.

So happy. And so eager to get away from there! Away from the school. Away from my nightmare.

Did I stop at my locker?

I must have stopped there because I had my jacket on when I burst outside. Into the frosty night air. I saw a tiny sliver of a moon high in a purple-black sky. I stopped for a second to breathe in the cold, fresh air.

Then I ran across the teachers' parking lot to the bike rack. I'd ridden my bike to school. And now I planned to put the pedal to the metal—to race all the way home.

"Yes!" So happy. I felt so happy, I could have *danced* all the way home.

I jumped on my bike. Grabbed the handlebars.

Whoa. Something wrong. A scraping sound.

I climbed off and glanced down. A flat tire. No. *Two* flat tires.

"Oh, wow," I murmured. How did that happen?

No big deal. I'll get the bike tomorrow, I decided. I started to jog across the parking lot, heading to the street. My sneaker felt loose. I squatted down to tie the shoe lace—and it ripped between my hands.

No problem, I told myself. I have plenty of shoelaces at home. I started walking, turned onto the sidewalk, crossed the street. Behind me I could hear shouts and cheers coming from the gym. I guessed that the game had started up again.

"Go, Stretch!" I murmured.

As I made my way down the next block it began to rain. Softly at first. But the wind picked up, and then the rain started coming down in sheets.

I zipped my jacket and leaned into the wind. But the rain drove me back, wave after wave of freezing water.

I heard a crackling sound nearby—and saw jagged, white lightning streak across the front yard across the street. A deafening boom of thunder shook the ground.

I pressed forward. Trees creaked and nearly bent sideways in the torrents of wind and rain. I couldn't move. I ducked under a broad-trunked tree for safety.

But a loud *crack* of lightning sent a tree branch crashing to my feet.

"Ohh!" I cried out. A close call!

I jumped over the fallen branch. Sharp pieces of the limb scratched my arm as I struggled to race away. Another jagged bolt of lightning crackled a few feet in front of me, sizzling over the wet grass.

Squinting through the downpour, I saw smoke snake over the lawn. The grass was burned black where the lightning had spread.

The wind shoved me backward. Sheet after sheet

of rain washed over me. I choked. Struggled to breathe.

And then . . . just beyond the rain . . . just beyond the heavy waves of dark water . . . I saw two glowing lights . . . two red eyes . . . like dark headlights . . . Two evil eyes, moving with me, watching me.

The Fate Master.

It wasn't a dream. I suddenly knew that my flat tires—the storm—the lightning, the pounding rain—it was all a show. A show of strength.

I staggered up my driveway. Slipped on the wet gravel. Sprawled facedown on the soaked stones.

"Nooooo . . ."

I struggled to my feet. Stumbled onto the front stoop.

A deafening, shattering crash made me spin around. I saw one of the oak trees in front of the house split in half. It appeared to move in slow motion. One half shivered but stayed upright. The other half of the broad, old tree came crashing onto the roof of the house.

Windows shattered. Roof tiles came sliding down.

I covered my head with one hand. And pushed the doorbell. Frantically pushed the bell. "Let me in! Mom! Dad!" I pounded on the front door with both fists.

Where were they?

The lights were all on. Why didn't they open the door?

A crash of thunder made me jump and cry out. Above the front stoop rainwater poured like a waterfall over the sides of the gutters. Waves of rain rattled the living room window and battered the bricks of the front wall.

"Let me in!" I screamed over another roar of thunder. I pounded the front door until my fist ached.

Then I heard a window slide open. I turned to our neighbor's house. Through the curtains of rain, I saw Mrs. Gillis poke her head out the bedroom window. She shouted something. But I couldn't hear her over the roar of rain.

"They're not home!" I finally heard her shout. "They had to go to the hospital, Luke."

"What? What did you say?" My heart jumped. Had I heard correctly?

"It's your dad. He fell down the stairs. He's okay. But they took him to the emergency room."

"No!" I cried. I beat my fists against the door. "No! No! No!"

The Fate Master was putting on a show for me. He was showing me who was boss. Giving me a little taste of what the rest of my life could be like.

"Okay!" I shouted, cupping my hands around my mouth. Water pounded me, washed over me, battered me against the house. “Okay—you win!” I screamed. “I’ll do it! I’ll do whatever you say!”

And I did.

The next morning I gave the skull to Stretch.

I found Stretch at his locker before school started. Giving him the yellow skull was the easiest thing in the world.

Stretch was leaning into his locker, searching the shelf for something. His backpack stood open on the floor. I pulled the skull from my jeans pocket—and dropped it into his backpack.

He didn't see anything. He didn't even know he had it.

"Hey, Stretch—how's it going?" I asked, trying to sound calm, natural. As if I hadn't just done something terrible to him. Something that would ruin his life forever.

"Yo—hey, Champ!" He slapped me a hard high five, so hard my hand stung. "How's your head, man? It looks as ugly as ever!" He laughed.

I stared at him. "My head?"

"That was a nasty collision," he said. "Your head must be hard as a rock. You feeling okay?"

"Yeah. Not bad," I replied.

Stretch snickered. "Well, thanks for letting me get some playing time." He started to close up his backpack.

I stared at the backpack, picturing the skull inside it. The skull I had passed on to Stretch. The tiny, red eyes were probably glowing again. Stretch was going to have a lot of good luck for a while. But then . . .

"Maybe you and I can practice together later," Stretch said, slamming his locker shut. "I can give you some more pointers. Make you look like you know what you're doing!"

"Yeah. Maybe," I said.

Stretch's expression turned serious. "Actually, you're not bad, man," he said. "I mean it. You are so improved. I mean, you're almost pretty good! Really."

I don't believe this! I thought. Stretch is actually paying me a compliment.

I shrugged. "It was just luck," I muttered.

Just luck. Ha ha.

"No way!" Stretch insisted. "Luck had nothing to do with it, man. It was hard work and skill. No kidding. It isn't luck. You're good!"

I swallowed hard. I suddenly felt like a total creep.

Stretch was being so nice to me. And what had I done to him? I just gave him a life of bad luck, a life of slavery to the Fate Master.

"Whoa. Forgot my science notebook," Stretch groaned. He dropped his backpack to the floor and turned to unlock his locker.

I stared down at the backpack, feeling dizzy, feeling sick.

What am I going to do? I asked myself. What am I going to do?

My bad luck continued all day.

I answered the wrong questions on my algebra test and got an F. Miss Wakely warned me that I'd have to do extra work if I didn't want to fail the course.

At lunch the milk in my milk carton was lumpy and sour. I didn't notice until I had gulped down a big mouthful. Then I nearly puked my guts up in front of everyone.

After lunch I started to comb my hair in the boys' room—and a huge clump came out on the comb. I gasped in horror and tugged out another clump of hair.

I'm going to lose all my hair! I realized.

As I hurried out of the bathroom, I caught my shirt on a nail and ripped one sleeve off. I was so upset, I bumped into Miss Wakely from behind. Her coffee cup flew out of her hand, and scalding hot coffee splashed all over her.

I found Hannah after school. She came rolling slowly down the hall in her wheelchair. Her foot was still bandaged. Her face was still covered in red blotches. And I saw that one of her eyes was swollen shut.

"Hannah—I've got to talk to you!" I cried.

"Did you pass it on?" she asked in a loud whisper.

"Huh?"

"I've lost my voice," she whispered. "Did you pass the skull on to Stretch? We've got to change our luck. I can barely see. My skin itches like crazy. I can barely talk. I—I can't go on like this, Luke."

"I've got to find the Fate Master," I said.

Hannah grabbed my torn shirtsleeve. "You've got to do what he said. You've got to obey him. It's our only chance."

"How do I find him?" I asked.

"He will find you," Hannah whispered. "He appears in places of bad luck. You know—broken mirrors, wherever the number thirteen is written."

"Come with me," I said. I led the way to my locker. I waved to some guys heading to the pool for swim team practice. I wanted to be with them. But this was more important.

"We've got to talk to the Fate Master," I told Hannah. "Maybe he'll come through my locker again."

Hannah groaned in pain as she wheeled herself behind me. "My foot hurts so much!" she whispered.

"He promised to end the bad luck," I said.

I turned the combination lock, then pulled open

my locker door. A burst of sour air choked the hall. I gagged, then held my breath.

"Look—" Hannah choked out. She pointed to the floor of the locker.

It was littered with dead birds. A pile of brown-and-gray sparrows, all dead and decaying.

"He left us a present," I murmured. "Where is he? Is he going to appear?"

We didn't have to wait long.

A few moments later I saw the glow of the red eyes at the back of the locker. And then the dark figure stepped over the pile of dead birds and floated out, hunched beneath the black hood.

"Have you done what I asked?" he rasped, the fiery eyes burning into mine. *"Have you given me a new slave?"*

"Yes," I replied, avoiding his stare. "That was our deal, right? And now will you stop torturing us? Will you end our bad luck as you promised?"

The hood bobbed up and down. *"No,"* he said softly.

Hannah and I both uttered cries of protest.

"Did you really think you could make a deal with the Fate Master?" he boomed. The open coat floated up like bat wings. *"I don't make bargains with anyone! I don't make promises! You will take whatever Fate dishes out!"*

"You promised—!" Hannah shrieked.

The evil figure snickered. *"First you enjoy good*

luck. Then you must pay for it. You cannot break the pattern. You should know that. You should know that you cannot bargain with Fate! You will pay for your good luck for the rest of your life!"

"No! Wait—! Wait!" Hannah pleaded, reaching up from the wheelchair, grasping at the black cloak, grasping frantically with both hands.

But the Fate Master spun around, swirling the foul air. He stomped heavily on the dead birds as he strode back into locker 13.

In a second he had vanished.

Dead birds littered the floor of the hall, the floor of my locker.

I turned to Hannah. Her shoulders heaved up and down. Loud sobs escaped her throat. "He promised. . . ."

"It's okay," I said softly. "I didn't keep my promise, either."

I pulled the yellow skull from my jeans pocket.

Hannah gasped. "You didn't give it to Stretch?"

I squeezed the skull in my fist. "Yes, I gave it to him. But I took it back before Stretch even saw it. I couldn't do it. Stretch was too nice to me. I—I couldn't. I couldn't ruin someone's life."

Hannah shook her head. Tears spilled from her swollen eyes. "Now what are we going to do, Luke? We're doomed. Now we don't stand a chance."

I bounced the basketball hard against the driveway. Drove toward the backboard and sent up a hook shot. It bounced off the rim, back into my hands. I spun hard and sent up a two-handed shot that dropped through the net.

Overhead, clouds covered the moon. The garage lights sent white cones of light over the driveway. Behind me, the house was dark except for a square of orange light from my bedroom window upstairs.

I glanced at the roof. Men had worked all day to repair the broken and missing shingles. The fallen tree had been hauled away. One window—broken in the storm—was still covered with cardboard.

All my fault, I realized. All the damage to the house was my fault.

My dad was walking with a cane. He had a badly sprained knee from his fall down the stairs. But he was okay . . . for now.

That was all my fault too, I knew.

All my bad luck.

I heaved the ball angrily at the backboard. It thudded high, bounced back to the driveway. I picked it up and shot it through the hoop.

Luck . . . luck . . . luck . . .

The word ran through my mind like an ugly chant.

And then I heard Stretch's words again. Stretch actually saying something nice to me: "Luck had nothing to do with it, Luke. It was hard work and skill."

Hard work and skill.

Not luck.

"You cannot break the pattern," the Fate Master had said. "First you have the good luck—then you pay for it."

The pattern. You cannot break the pattern.

Not luck. Hard work and skill.

I shot the ball again. Dribbled, then shot again. Even though it was a cold, frosty night, sweat poured down my forehead. I wanted to work harder. Harder.

And as I practiced, those words repeated and repeated in my mind. And I knew what I had to do. I knew the only way I could end the bad luck for Hannah and for me.

The only way I could defeat the Fate Master.

I shot again. Again. I moved to the foul line and put up several foul shots.

I didn't stop when I saw the kitchen light flash on. The back door swung open. Dad stepped into the yard, wearing his bathrobe, leaning on his cane.

"Luke—what are you doing?" he called. "It's after eleven o'clock!"

"Practicing," I said, sending up another jump shot.

Walking unsteadily, he came up to the edge of the driveway. "But—it's so late. Why are you doing this?"

"I'm going to win *without* luck!" I replied. I sent up another shot and watched it drop through the hoop. "I'm going to win with skill! I shouted. "I can break the pattern! I can win without luck."

And then, without realizing it, I was screaming at the top of my lungs: "I DON'T NEED LUCK! I DON'T NEED LUCK!"

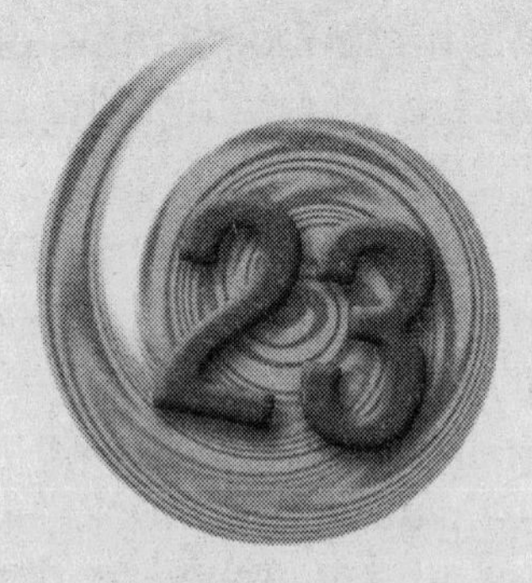

My plan was simple. Maybe too simple.

But I had to give it a try.

I didn't tell it to Hannah. She was pretty much destroyed. I didn't want to give her any more to worry about.

I knew I didn't have much time—maybe a day or two at the most.

As soon as the Fate Master discovered that I still had the skull, that I hadn't passed it on to Stretch, he would come after me full force.

My plan?

It was to break the pattern.

To win. To win big. To have a major success. Without luck. Without needing any good luck.

If I could win with my own hard work, with my own skill, my own talent—it would be a defeat for the Fate Master. I would break his rule. I would break the pattern.

And maybe . . . just maybe that would free Hannah and me.

And that's why I practiced on my driveway. Practiced in the dark, in the cold until after midnight. Hard work and skill.

Hard work and skill.

Shawnee Valley played Forest Grove this afternoon. The last game of the season.

My last chance to win without luck.

As I changed into my team uniform, I knew I had to be great. I had to be a winner today. I had to win the game for my team.

And if I did?

If I did, maybe the nightmare would be over.

I was so nervous, I had to lace up my sneakers three times. I kept knotting them up. My fingers just wouldn't work.

"Go, Squires! Go, Squires!"

Guys were pounding their fists on the lockers, shouting, jumping up and down, getting pumped, getting ready.

Stretch gave me a playful slap as he jogged past. "Try not to bump heads today, Champ! We gonna beat these clowns?"

I flashed him a thumbs-up. "They're dead meat!" I shouted.

I tucked in my jersey, slammed the gym locker shut, and trotted out into the gym. I blinked under the bright lights. A big crowd nearly filled the bleachers. They were stamping their feet in time to some marching music over the loudspeaker.

I searched for Hannah but didn't see her.

The last game of the year, I thought as I picked up a basketball from the rack. My last chance . . .

I swallowed hard, trying to force down my fear.

Was the Fate Master here? Did he know that I lied to him? That I didn't give the skull to Stretch?

I don't care about that, I told myself. I'm going to be a winner today without his good luck.

I'm going to break the pattern.

I'm going to break the Fate Master!

I dribbled up to Coach Bendix. He slapped me on the shoulder as I passed. "Have a great game, Luke!" he called. "Keep it slow and steady. Remember—just focus. Focus."

"Okay, Coach," I called. "I'm ready. I feel good. Real strong. I think I'm going to—"

I felt a strong blast of cold air. It swept through the gym, like an invisible ocean wave.

And then I saw Coach's expression change very suddenly. He was grinning at me, flashing me a thumbs-up. And then his hand came down. His face went slack. His eyes appeared to fade, to glaze over as if a curtain had been drawn over them.

As if he'd been hypnotized or something.

"Hey, Luke," he said, motioning me back to him. He frowned, narrowing his eyes at me.

"What is it?" I asked, keeping up my dribble.

"Take the bench," he ordered, pointing to the team bench with his whistle.

"Huh?" I gaped at him.

"The bench," he repeated, his face a blank now, his eyes vacant, dull. "You can't play today."

"Hey—no way!" I protested. "What do you *mean*? I've *got* to play!"

He shook his head. "You can't play today, Luke. Your concussion—remember? I need a doctor's note. Have you been examined? You can't play until you're examined."

My mouth hung open. "Coach . . . I've been practicing so hard. Please. You've got to let me in the game today," I pleaded. My heart pounded so hard, I felt dizzy. My head throbbed. "Coach . . . I *have* to play. It's the last game."

He shook his head. "Sorry." He motioned to the bench. "We have to follow the rules."

Whose rules? I thought bitterly. The Fate Master's rules?

Coach Bendix gazed at me with those glazed, blank eyes. "Sorry. You've already played your last game, Luke."

"But—but—" I sputtered.

"You'll get 'em next year!" he said. He blew his whistle. "Stretch—you're in! You're playing the whole game!"

I stood there. I didn't move. I stood in the middle of the floor with my hands on my waist. Waiting for my heart to stop racing. Waiting for my legs to stop trembling.

Then I turned and slowly trudged to the bench.

I'd lost today. Score one round for the Fate Master.

No way I could break the pattern today. I was a loser today.

But I wasn't finished. I could still win.

If I had time . . .

“Give the skull to Stretch,” Hannah pleaded. “Maybe the Fate Master will go easy on us.”

It was the next day. We were huddled at the back of the lunchroom. I could see Stretch laughing and kidding around with his friends at a table near the front. The Squires had won the game by two points, and Stretch had been a hero.

“I can’t do it,” I said, shaking my head. “Besides, you heard what the Fate Master said. He doesn’t make deals. It won’t help to pass it to Stretch.”

Hannah let out a sigh. She had her head buried in her hands. “Then what are we going to do?”

“I’ll find a way to defeat him,” I said. I bit into my ham sandwich. “Hey—!” I felt something hard.

“Oh no,” I moaned. I spit out a tooth.

In a panic I moved my tongue around the inside of my mouth. “My teeth,” I groaned. “They’re all loose. I’m going to lose all my teeth.”

Hannah didn’t lift her head. She whispered something, too low for me to hear.

"I've got to go," I said, jumping up. "I have some ideas, Hannah. Don't give up hope. I have some ideas."

I ran past Stretch's table, where the guys were laughing and blowing straw wrappers at each other. Stretch called out to me, but I didn't stop.

I made my way to the computer lab. The door was closed. I pulled it open and burst breathlessly into the brightly lit room.

"Mrs. Coffey? Mrs. Coffey? It's me—Luke!"

I felt another tooth swing loose in my mouth. I gritted my teeth, trying to press it down into place.

A chubby young man I'd never seen before came out of the supply room. He had short black hair on top of a round, pudgy face, and bright red cheeks. He looked like an apple with eyes! He wore a red plaid shirt over black denims.

"Is Mrs. Coffey here?" I demanded. "I need to talk to her."

He set down the disk drive he was carrying. "She's gone," he said.

"You mean she went to lunch?" I asked.

He shook his round head. "No. She left school. She got another job."

"I—I know," I stammered. "But I thought—"

"I'm Ron Handleman," he said. "I'm taking over the computer lab. Do you have a class with me?"

"Uh . . . no," I said. "But I have a project I was supposed to show Mrs. Coffey. She was going to send it to someone who might put it in a show. It's computer animation, you see. I've been working on it for two years and . . . and . . ." In my panic the words poured out of me. I had to stop to take a breath.

"Slow down," Mr. Handleman said. "She probably left me a note about it. She left me a stack of notes." He glanced around the cluttered worktable. "I put them somewhere."

How could Mrs. Coffey leave without seeing my project? I asked myself. How could she do that to me?

Didn't she realize how important it was? This could be my big triumph. If my computer animation is accepted for a show—because of my hard work, *only* because of my skill and hard work—it would break the pattern. It might defeat the Fate Master.

Didn't she *realize*?

"Uh . . . can you look at my computer animation?" I asked.

Mr. Handleman's cheeks grew redder. "When?"

"Tonight?" I asked, my heart pounding.

"Well . . . I don't think so," he replied. "Not tonight. I mean, this is my first day. I have so much to do here. Maybe next week . . . "

"No!" I screamed. "You have to look at it! Please! It's very important!"

"I'd love to see it," he said, picking up the disk drive, starting across the room with it. "But I have to get organized. Maybe . . ."

"Please!" I cried. "Find Mrs. Coffey's note. We've got to get it to the man who's putting together the computer art show. Please!"

He narrowed his eyes at me. He probably thought I was crazy.

But I didn't care. I needed a victory. I knew there wasn't much time.

"Okay," Mr. Handleman said finally. "Bring it in first thing tomorrow morning. I'll try to look at it during lunch."

Not good enough. Tomorrow might be too late, I realized.

"How late will you be here this afternoon?" I asked breathlessly.

"Pretty late," he replied. "Since it's my first day, I—"

"I'll run home after school and get it," I said. "I'll bring it to you before you leave tonight. Could you . . . I mean, would you look at it this afternoon? Please?"

"Okay, I guess. I'll be here till at least five," he said.

"Yesss!" I cried, pumping my fist in the air. I turned and raced out of the computer lab.

I can win! I told myself. I can defeat the Fate Master. My animation project is good. I know it is. I've worked for two years on it. I've put so much hard work into it.

I don't need luck. I don't need good luck at all.

After school I ran all the way home. I burst into the kitchen, tossed down my backpack, and started to my room. I stopped halfway to the stairs when I heard voices from the living room.

"Luke—is that you?" Mom called.

Mom and Dad were both there, sitting in the dark. Dad leaned heavily on his cane. Mom had her hands clasped tightly in her lap.

I stopped in the living room doorway. "Why are you both home so early?" I asked.

"I had to come home. I couldn't work," Dad said softly. "That fall I took. It was worse than we thought. Looks like I'm going to need surgery."

"Oh, no," I muttered. My fault. It was all my fault.

But I didn't really have time to talk to them. I had to get to my computer. I wanted to check out the animation one more time before I made a copy for Mr. Handleman. Then I had to rush back to school.

"But why are you sitting in the dark?" I asked. "Why don't you turn on some lights?"

"We can't," Mom said, shaking her head. "There's some kind of trouble with the power lines to our block. The electricity is off. We have no power. No power at all."

I let out a horrified scream. "Nooooo! My computer!"

"You'll have to wait till the power comes back on," Dad said.

"But—but—" I sputtered.

"We're having so much bad luck all of a sudden," Dad murmured.

"We may have to leave the house tonight," Mom said, sighing unhappily. "Without electricity we have no heat. We may have to check into a hotel or something."

"Oh, no." I tugged at my hair. A big clump of it came out in my hand.

I was losing my hair. Losing my teeth. How could I fight back? How?

"He can't do this to me!" I screamed. "He can't! He can't!" I turned and grabbed the banister and pulled myself up the stairs.

"Luke? What are you saying?"

"Where are you going?"

I didn't answer. I dived into my room and slammed the door shut behind me.

Breathing hard, I stared at my computer. Stared at the dark monitor screen.

Useless. Totally useless.

Frustrated, I kicked the side of my desk. "Owww!" I didn't mean to kick it that hard. Sharp pain throbbed up my leg, up my side.

"Oh, wait." I suddenly remembered. I already made a copy!

Yes! I made a backup copy of my project. On my Zip drive. Yes!

I fumbled frantically through the pile of disks on my desk. And grabbed the Zip disk.

I still have a chance, I told myself. The Fate Master thought he shut me down. But I still have a chance.

I stuffed the disk into my jacket pocket. I hurled myself down the stairs two at a time. "Bye! I have to go back to school!" I shouted to my parents.

"Why?"

"What's going on, Luke? We need you here."

"Hey—come back and explain!"

I heard their cries, but I burst out the front door and kept running.

"I'll stop the bad luck," I said out loud. "I'll stop it. I'll stop the Fate Master—now!"

I found Mr. Handleman in the computer lab, leaning over a keyboard, typing an e-mail message.

He spun around when I shouted hi to him.

I held up the disk. "Here it is! Please! You've got to check it out!"

He motioned for me to sit down next to him. "I spoke to the producer of the computer show," he said. "He called me this afternoon. He said that if I liked your animation, I should send it over to him right away."

"Excellent!" I cried. "That's great news!"

"Aren't you going to take your coat off?"

"No," I answered breathlessly. I shoved the disk into the Zip drive. "No time. You have to see this. Right away."

He laughed. "Slow down. Take a deep breath."

"I'll breathe *after* you see it!" I said.

He leaned back in his chair and used his hands as a headrest. "You've been working on this for two years?"

I nodded.

I found the file in the disk directory and double-clicked it. "Here goes," I said. I was so nervous, the mouse trembled in my hand. My chest was so tight, it felt about to burst.

Is it possible to *explode* from excitement? I leaned forward to watch.

The screen was solid black. "It's starting now," I whispered.

I stared at the black screen, waiting for the bright burst of color at the beginning.

Waiting . . .

Finally a dim glow spread over the screen.

Two circles of light. Two red circles glowed in the center of the darkness.

Two red, glowing eyes.

The eyes stared out, unblinking, unmoving. Blank, round circles of shimmering red.

Mr. Handleman cleared his throat. His eyes remained locked on the monitor screen. "Are those eyes?" he asked. "Do they move or anything?"

I opened my mouth to answer, but no sound came out.

I stared frozen in horror at the glowing eyes. The evil eyes.

And knew I had been defeated again.

Mr. Handelman's cheeks were bright red now. "Is this all there is?" he asked.

"Yes," I whispered. "That's all."

My project was gone. My two years of work were lost.

The fiery eyes stared out at me in triumph.

I climbed to my feet and slumped out of the room.

I trudged down the empty hall, head down, hands shoved deep in my pockets. I've lost, I realized. I'm a loser forever now. Hannah and me both. Bad luck for the rest of our lives.

I turned a corner—and almost bumped into Coach Swanson. "Hey, Luke—how's it going?" he asked.

I muttered a reply under my breath.

"I was going to call you tonight," he said. "Andy Mason is sick. You have to swim in his place tomorrow."

I raised my head. "Huh? Swim?" I had nearly forgotten that I was on the swim team.

"See you after school at the pool," the coach said. "Good luck."

I'll need it, I thought glumly.

But then I realized I was being given one more chance.

One more chance to win *without* luck. One more chance to defeat Fate.

One *last* chance . . .

The next morning I wore a baseball cap to school so no one could see the bald patches on my head. When I brushed my teeth that morning, another tooth came sliding out between my lips.

My tongue was covered with hard, white bumps. My arms and legs itched. I was starting to get the same red blotches on my skin as Hannah.

Somehow I made it through the school day. All I could think about was the swim team race. Was there any way that I might win? That I might break the pattern and win the race and defeat the Fate Master?

I didn't have much hope. But I knew I had to try. I knew I had to give it everything I had left.

A few seconds after I lowered myself into the pool to warm up, Coach Swanson's whistle rang out, echoing off the tile walls. "Practice laps, everyone!" the coach shouted. "Do them half-speed. Let's see some warm-up laps."

At the other end of the pool I saw Stretch kick off and begin swimming with steady, strong strokes. I did a surface dive and started to follow him. The warm water felt good on my itchy skin.

I kicked hard. Picked up speed.

As I raised my head to suck in a deep breath, the water suddenly churned hard.

I swallowed a big mouthful. Started to choke.

I sputtered, struggling to clear my throat, struggling to breathe.

And then, to my horror, my stomach heaved hard. "Guuurrrrrp." My lunch came hurling up.

I couldn't hold it back. I vomited a thick, dark puddle into the clear water.

"Ooh, gross!"

"Sick!"

"Yuck! Oh, wow—he's puking his guts up!"

A sick, sour smell rose up from the water. I heard kids shouting and groaning in disgust.

And then I heard Coach Swanson's whistle. And the coach shouting at me: "You're outta there, Luke! Get out. You're sick. You're not going to swim today!"

No, I thought. This can't happen again. This is my last chance.

"Coach, I'm okay!" I shouted. "I just . . . swallowed some water. I can swim—really!"

Coach Swanson glanced around the pool. Andy Mason was in street clothes. Joe Bork, the other alternate, didn't show up.

"You've got to let me swim!" I pleaded.

The coach shrugged his shoulders. "There's no one else. I guess I've got no choice."

I'm going to do this, I thought. I'm going to win today. I'm going to do whatever it takes to win.

The race got off to a good start. I did a speed dive at the whistle and found myself gliding, stroking easily, in the lead.

Swimming steadily, keeping up a smooth rhythm, I stayed in the lead until the waves began.

Waves? They tossed up in front of me, rolled rapidly toward me, splashed over me. Wave after wave. Pushing me back. Slowing my pace.

Stroking harder to keep my rhythm, I turned to the side and glanced at the other swimmers. The pool was smooth, the water flat for them.

The waves were just for me! A strong current pushed at me, slowing me, shoving me back.

I ducked under the waves. Let them splash and roll over me. And swam harder.

Harder.

"Oh!" Something brushed my leg.

I felt something curl around an ankle. Something bumped my waist. I felt something slide around my knee.

With another gasp I turned—and saw the gray-green creatures. Eels? Were they *eels*?

Wrapping around my legs. Twining over my waist.

Long, fat eels. The water churned with them!

I cried out.

I saw the other swimmers, gliding swiftly through clear water. They didn't even notice my dark, churning water. They didn't even see the gleaming, wet creatures slithering between my legs. Tightening around my ankles, my legs.

Slapping me . . . slapping me hard . . . slapping me back.

"No!" I burst free. I kept swimming.

Into thick pink clusters of jellyfish. The jellyfish ballooned around me. Stung my arms. Stung my legs. Prickled the skin of my back.

I cried out in pain. The sticky creatures swarmed over me, stinging, stinging me again and again.

I could see the other swimmers moving smoothly, ahead of me now. Gliding in smooth, clear waters as I felt jolt after jolt of pain from the billowing jellyfish that clustered over me.

I slapped the water. Slapped and kicked.

And let out another cry of pain as the water sizzled and boiled. Scalding hot now. It steamed and bubbled. And my skin burned. My skin is going to burn right off me, I thought, struggling to breathe. Struggling to keep my arms moving through the scalding steam. Kicking . . . kicking hard . . .

The other swimmers ahead of me now. Moving so speedily, so steadily . . .

I shut my eyes and swam. You're not going to beat me! I thought. I'm going to win . . . going to win.

And the thought gave me a final surge of energy.

I shot forward to the wall. Plunged like a speeding torpedo to the finish.

My hand hit the wall. I slapped the wall.

Gasping . . . gasping . . . my chest heaving in agony . . . And knew that I had lost.

Too slow. Too slow.

I knew that I had lost again.

Water poured down my face. I shut my eyes and struggled to catch my breath.

I heard a loud whistle. Then I felt a hand on my shoulder. A slap. "Way to go, Luke!"

I opened my eyes to see the coach. He grabbed my hand and pumped it hard. Then he slapped me a high five. "You won! You came from behind! What a race, Luke! Check out the time! You set a school record!"

"Huh? I did? I won?"

He helped me out of the pool. Guys were cheering and yelling congratulations.

But the cheering was cut short by a deafening cry from the middle of the pool. A shrill wail that rose like an ambulance siren. Higher . . . higher . . . until I was forced to cover my ears.

And then a mountain of water rose up from the pool. Red and steaming like a volcano. The water rose up—higher, higher—like a bubbling, boiling red tidal wave. And all the while the deafening wail rang out with it.

Everyone was screaming. We all were screaming.

And then, as suddenly as it rose up, the molten, red mountain collapsed back into the pool. Collapsed with a soft splash. The pool was flat and smooth again. And silent. Silent except for our stunned gasps and cries.

I turned to see Hannah running along the side of the pool. Hannah out of her wheelchair. Running. Running wildly, waving her arms excitedly, laughing, her red hair flying behind her.

"Luke—you did it! We're free! You defeated Fate! Luke—you defeated Fate!"

But it wasn't enough. Not enough for me.

I changed into my street clothes in seconds. Then I dragged Hannah down the hall to my locker. Locker 13.

I stopped at the janitor's closet. And I grabbed a huge sledgehammer.

Hannah cheered as I raised the sledgehammer to the locker, and smashed it . . . smashed it . . . smashed it.

Working feverishly, I pried the battered locker from the wall. Kicked it onto its side. Raised the sledgehammer again. Smashed it . . . crushed it . . . smashed it.

The battered locker door swung open. I heard a low groan from deep inside.

Hannah and I both leaped back as a skull rolled out onto the floor.

Not a tiny skull. A human-sized skull with glowing red eyes.

The eyes glowed for only a few seconds. Then the skull uttered a final groan, a groan of agony, of defeat. And the eyes faded to darkness. Empty darkness.

I took a deep breath. Ran up to it—and kicked the skull down the hall.

"Goal!" Hannah yelled.

We walked out of the school building arm in arm. Into the bright afternoon sunlight.

I took a long, deep breath. The air smelled so fresh, so sweet.

The houses, the trees, the sky—they all looked so beautiful.

I stopped at the bottom of the sidewalk. And bent down to pick something up.

"Hey, check it out!" I showed it to Hannah. "Is this my lucky day?" I cried. "I found a penny!"

ABOUT THE AUTHOR

R.L. STINE says he has a great job. "My job is to give kids the CREEPS!" With his scary books, R.L. has terrified kids all over the world. He has sold over 300 million books, making him the best-selling children's author in history.

These days, R.L. is dishing out new frights in his series THE NIGHTMARE ROOM. When he isn't working, he likes to read old mysteries, watch *SpongeBob Squarepants* on TV, and take his dog, Nadine, for long walks around New York City, where he lives with his wife, Jane, and son, Matthew.

"I love taking my readers to scary places," R.L. says. "Do you know the scariest place of all? It's your MIND!"

Take a look at what's ahead in

THE NIGHTMARE ROOM #3

Liar, Liar

"Hey, check it out. A fortune-teller!" Jilly said. She pointed to a small, black tent that stood beside an ice cream cart. "Can we do it? I love fortune-tellers!"

"No way," I said. "They make me nervous. I don't even like watching them in movies."

"Come on, Maggie. It's your birthday," her sister Jackie said, pulling me to the tent. "You have to have your fortune told on your birthday."

"Let's see what the fortune-teller says about you and Glen!" Judy, the third sister teased.

"I don't think so," I said.

But as usual, they didn't give me a choice. A few seconds later, we were standing at the doorway to the dark tent.

"We'll all have our fortunes told," Jackie said. "My treat."

"This is so cool!" Jilly whispered. "Do you think it's a real psychic? Do you think she can really tell the future?"

The three sisters started into the tent. I held back, staring at the red and black, hand-lettered sign: MISS ELIZABETH. FORTUNE-TELLER. ONE DOLLAR.

I suddenly realized that my heart was racing.

Why do I feel so weird? I wondered. *Why do I have such a bad feeling about this?*

I followed my friends into the tent. The air inside felt hot and steamy. Two electric lanterns on the back tent wall splashed gray light over the fortune-teller's small table.

Miss Elizabeth sat hunched with her elbows on the table, head in her hands, staring into a red glass ball. She didn't look up as we stepped inside. I couldn't tell if she was concentrating on the red ball, or if she was asleep.

The tent was completely bare, except for her table and two wooden chairs, and a large black-and-white poster of a human hand. The hand was divided into sections. There was a lot of writing all over the poster, too small for me to read in the smoky, gray light.

As she stared into the red glass ball, the fortune-teller muttered to herself. She was a middle-aged woman, slender, with bony arms poking out from the sleeves of her red dress, and very large, pale white hands. Squinting into the light, I saw that the polish on her long fingernails matched the red of her dress.

"Hel-lo?" Jackie called, breaking the silence.

Miss Elizabeth finally looked up. She was kind of pretty. She had big, round black eyes and dramatic red-lipsticked lips. Her hair was long and wavy, solid black except for a wide white streak down the middle.

Her eyes moved from one of us to the other. She didn't smile. "Walter, we have visitors," she announced in a hoarse, scratchy voice.

I glanced around, searching for Walter.

"Walter is my late husband," the fortune-teller announced. "He helps me channel information from the spirits."

Jackie and I exchanged glances.

"We'd like you to tell our fortunes," Jilly said.

Miss Elizabeth nodded solemnly. "One dollar each." She held out her long, pale hand. "Four dollars please."

Jackie fumbled in her bag and pulled out four crumpled dollar bills. She handed them to the fortune-teller, who shoved them into a pocket of her red dress.

"Who wants to go first?" Again, her eyes moved slowly over our faces.

"I'll go," Jilly volunteered. She dropped into the chair across the table from Miss Elizabeth.

The fortune-teller lowered her head again to gaze into the red ball. "Walter, bring me the words of the spirit world about this young woman."

I suddenly felt a chill at the back of my neck. I knew I shouldn't be frightened. The woman had to be a fake—right? Otherwise, she wouldn't be working in a tacky carnival like this one.

But she was so serious. So solemn. She didn't seem to be putting on an act.

Or was I just being gullible again?

Now she took Jilly's hand. She pulled it up close to her face and began to study Jilly's palm. Muttering to herself, she moved her long finger back and forth, following the lines of the palm, tracing them with her bright red fingernail.

Jackie leaned close to me. "This is cool," she whispered.

Judy sighed. "This is going to take forever."

Jackie raised a finger to her lips and motioned for Judy to shush.

The woman studied Jilly's palm for a long time, squeezing the hand as she gazed at it, murmuring to Walter in the red glass ball. Finally, she raised her eyes to Jilly. "You are artistic," she said in her scratchy voice.

"Yes!" Jilly declared.

"You are a . . . dancer," Miss Elizabeth continued. "You study the dance. You are a hard worker."

"Whoa. I don't believe this!" Jilly gushed. "How do you know—?"

"You have much talent," the fortune-teller murmured, ignoring Jilly's question. "Much talent. But sometimes . . . I see . . . your artistic side gets in the way of your practical side. You are . . . you are . . ."

She shut her eyes. "Help me, Walter," she whispered. Then she opened her eyes again and raised them to Jilly's palm. "You are a very social person. Your friends mean a lot to you. Especially . . . boy friends."

Jackie and Judy laughed. Jilly flashed them an angry scowl. "I—I don't believe this," she told the fortune-teller. "You have everything right!"

"It is my gift," Miss Elizabeth replied softly.

"Will I make the new dance company?" Jilly asked her. "Try-outs are next week. Can you tell me if I will be accepted?"

Miss Elizabeth stared into the glass ball. "Walter?" she whispered.

I held my breath, waiting for the answer. Jilly and I were both trying out for the dance company. And I knew there was only room for one of us.

"Walter can find no answer," the fortune-teller told Jilly. "He only groans." She let go of Jilly's hand.

"He—groaned?" Jilly asked. "Why?"

"Your time is up," Miss Elizabeth said. She motioned to us. "Who is next?"

Jackie shoved Judy forward. Judy dropped into the chair and held her hand out to Miss Elizabeth.

Jilly came running over to join Jackie and me at the edge of the tent. "Isn't she *amazing*?" she whispered.

"Yes, she is," I had to admit. How did she know so many true things about Jilly? I was beginning to believe Miss Elizabeth really had powers.

And now I didn't feel afraid or nervous. I was eager to see what the fortune-teller would say about me.

She squeezed Judy's hand and gazed deep into Judy's dark eyes. "You have great love in you," she announced. "Great love for . . . animals."

Judy gasped. "Y-yes!"

"You care for them. You work . . ."

"Yes," Judy said. "I work in an animal shelter after school. That's amazing!"

Miss Elizabeth ran a red fingernail down Judy's palm. "You also have an animal that you care about very much. A dog . . . No. A cat."

"Yes. My cat. Plumper."

Judy turned to us, her face filled with astonishment. "Do you *believe* this? She's right about *everything*!"

"I know! It's so cool!" Jilly exclaimed. She swept back her blond hair with a toss of her head. She kept bouncing up and down. She seemed too excited to stand still.

The fortune-teller spent a few more minutes with Judy. She told Judy that she would have a long, successful life. She said Judy would have a big family someday.

"Of kids? Of animals?" Judy asked.

Miss Elizabeth didn't answer.

Next came Jackie's turn. Once again, Miss Elizabeth was right on target with everything she said. "Wow," Jackie kept muttering. "Wow."

Finally, I found myself in the chair across from the fortune-teller. Suddenly, I felt so nervous. My mouth was dry. My legs were shaking.

Miss Elizabeth looked older from close up.

When she smiled at me, the thick makeup on her face cracked. Tiny drops of sweat glistened at her hairline.

"What is your name?" she asked in a whisper.

"Maggie," I told her.

She nodded solemnly and took my hand. She raised my palm close to her face and squinted down at it in the gray light.

I held my breath. And waited. What would she see?

She squeezed my hand. Brought it closer to her face.

And then . . . then . . . her eyes bulged wide. She let out a loud gasp.

With a violent jerk, she tossed my hand away.

And jumped to her feet. Her chair fell behind her, clattering to the tent floor.

She stared at me—stared in open-mouthed horror.

And then she screamed:

"*Get OUT! Get AWAY from here!!*"

"Huh? Wait—" I choked out.

"*Get OUT! You bring EVIL! You bring EVIL with you! Get OUT of here!*"